THE NESTER

All his life, Rod Devers had wanted only one thing—his own spread.

To get it, he hired his gun to the highest bidder. When he had it he hung up his gun.

Then Egan Valley exploded into range war. But Rod refused to take either side until he stood alone, deserted by friends as well as the girl he loved.

Then once again he strapped on his gun and went out to take on both sides—knowing that one or the other would kill him.

THE NESTER

John S. Daniels

This hardback edition 1999
by Chivers Press
by arrangement with
Golden West Literary Agency

Copyright ® 1953 by Wayne D. Overholser
Copyright © renewed 1981 by Wayne D. Overholser

ISBN 0 7540 8074 9

British Library Cataloguing in Publication Data available

Printed and bound in Great Britain by
Redwood Books, Trowbridge, Wiltshire

Chapter I

To CHERISH an ambition when it is a vague dream is one thing, to struggle with it in terms of sweat and tired muscles in the shadow of failure is another. As Rod Devers dug out the spring that had been mudded up the night before and repaired the pole enclosure which surrounded it, he wondered moodily if he had been smart or just plain stupid in starting his Rocking R here along the northern edge of Egan Valley. But smart or not, he knew that if he hadn't settled here, he would have tried it somewhere else.

As long as he could remember, Rod had been obsessed by the ambition to own a spread. That was why he had hired his gun and bargained with death for the highest wages he could get, saving his money until he had enough to buy a small herd.

He had been twenty-four when he had come to the valley three years ago, content to hang up his gun. He'd found what he wanted, a flowing spring and pines and a hay meadow below the cabin site, so exactly what he wanted that he had the weird feeling some unseen power had guided him here.

The day was hot even for late June, and sweat made a constant drip down Rod's face as he worked. By the time he was done, the sun was low in the west and shadows had crawled across the clearing until they reached the spring. He tossed his hammer into the grass, sourly considering the fact that this was the fourth time the spring had been mudded up. There had been other things, too, little pestering things that got under a man's skin.

The knowledge that he would have been all right if he had been content to wait didn't sweeten his temper. He hadn't been getting ahead fast enough, not fast enough to marry Doll Nance anyhow, and that was why he'd got his tail in a crack. If a man had enough pride to be worth a damn, he'd be able to support a woman or he wouldn't marry her. But Doll was a little short on patience.

Early in the spring Rod had borrowed two thousand dollars

1

from Jason Abbot, the Poplar City horse trader, giving his herd as security, and he'd used the money to buy a herd of two-year-old heifers in Warner Valley. Right now two thousand dollars looked as big as a million.

The note was due the first of September, and although Abbot had promised Rod more time if he needed it, the man might not keep his word. Beef prices had dropped, and what they would be in the fall was anybody's guess. It was that uncertainty which had planted the suspicion in Rod's mind that Abbot was responsible for these "accidents," hoping to discourage Rod so he'd sell his original herd and the heifers for about fifty cents on the dollar and get out with what he could.

Rod was not aware that his neighbor, Sam Kane, had ridden out of the pines above the spring until the man called, "Howdy, Rod."

Startled, Rod turned. He said, "Howdy, Sam," and waited while Kane rode down the slope to the spring.

Reining up, Kane nodded at the broken poles on the ground that Rod had replaced. He said, "Looks like it happened again."

"Some damned horse leaned too hard," Rod said.

Kane swung down, his red, square face grim. "Got any notion who's doing it?"

Kane might have done it himself, for he was one of Abbot's best friends. Or Todd Shannon who lived west of Rod's Rocking R and would do anything for a quick dollar. It might even be Abbot and the two boys who rode for him. But these were all guesses, based on nothing more than Rod's vague uneasiness about the money he owed Abbot.

Rod shook his head. "No notion at all."

Kane leaned on the top pole, staring at the water that was forming a new channel in the mud below the spring. He was a chunky man twenty years older than Rod, hard-working, bull-headed, and given to forcing his opinion on his neighbors. His SK lay a couple of miles to the east. Rod had ridden with him on roundup; they had swapped work at haying time, but Rod had promised himself they'd never do it again. To Sam Kane there were only two ways of doing anything, his way and the wrong way.

"Your trouble's just starting," Kane said ominously. "You heard about Karl Hermann coming?"

"I ain't heard nothing else since we knew he was looking over his layouts on the Malheur."

"You're a mite proddy," Kane murmured. "Anything else happen to sour your temper?"

"The fence between me and Todd Shannon's place was down again last night and his cows got into my hay field. A little more of that and I won't be cutting no hay this year."

Kane straightened and putting his back to the poles, pulled a brier pipe out of his pocket. "Want to know who's doing it?"

"You bet I want to know."

Kane filled his pipe and slipped the tobacco can into his pocket. "Chances are you'll get sore."

"I'll listen."

"How well do you know your brother George?"

"If you think George . . ."

"Yeah, I figured you'd take it that way," Kane said.

"Me'n George get along pretty well," Rod said, "providing there's a few miles between us which there usually is, but there's one thing about George. He ain't sneaky."

"Maybe you know." Kane shrugged. "The point is trouble don't always start big. Like you see a little cloud in the sky and pretty soon you've got a hell of a storm on your hands. Well, I rode over to see where you stand."

"You ought to know without me telling you," Rod snapped.

Kane shook his head. "Not with your brother rodding Spade for Karl Hermann. Worth a hundred million dollars, Hermann is, but he ain't satisfied. Once he gets a toehold on a range, he keeps working on it till he's got it all."

"You've been listening to Jason Abbot."

"You'd best do some listening, too." Kane lighted his pipe and pulled hard on it for a moment. "You'n me and Otto Larkin and the rest of us are nesters to a man like Hermann. We're just squatting, so Hermann will claim that the whole damned valley north of Spade is open range."

Impatient with the man's fears, Rod said, "You don't know what he'll claim."

Kane took the pipe out of his mouth, a bitter, worried man. "If you wasn't important, Rod, I wouldn't bother riding over here. There's some like your neighbor Todd Shannon who ain't worth a damn. They'll move on, but I figure you're one who'll stick."

Rod stared at Kane's grim face, not sure what the man was actually driving at. He said irritably, "Sure I'll stick, but I've got my own row to hoe, and I'm pretty damned busy hoeing it."

"You're cranky as hell today," Kane said plaintively, "but there's one more thing I'm gonna say. You're a good man to have on our side if it comes to a fight . . ."

"But we ain't got a fight yet. Not with Hermann."

"We will soon as he gets here. I'm just laying this out the way I see it. It's the little fellows like you'n me who'll stick it out through the bad years and the good ones that makes a country amount to something. We'll fight for what's ours, and to hell with Karl Hermann."

"You're overlooking one thing," Rod said. "I ain't found out who I'm fighting."

Exasperated, Kane shouted, "I tell you it's Hermann and your brother George. We want you on our side and they want you to get clean out of the country so you won't be on our side. Everybody knows you've been a gunfighter. That's the reason they keep pestering you. They figure you'll stand about so much and then you'll light a shuck out of the country."

Kane had let his pipe go cold in his hand. He was watching Rod's lean face closely as if trying to read his mind. Rod picked up his shovel and hammer, the thought striking him that Jason Abbot might have sent Kane here with this cock and bull yarn about George.

"All right," Rod said. "Go tell Abbot you spoke your piece."

"He's got nothing to do with me being here," Kane said sullenly. "It's time somebody was taking a lead, so I'm doing it. We're having a meeting in the Palace tonight to organize. When Hermann gets here, we'll tell him we're working together and we'll swap slug for slug. I want you to be at that meeting."

"No," Rod said. "I don't want no part of it."

"Then you're against us." Kane knocked his pipe out and put it into his pocket. "Looks like Hermann sent you here in the first place."

Rod fought his temper for a moment, wanting to kick Kane off the ranch, a desire which was balanced by the knowledge that it wouldn't do any good. Probably it was the very thing Abbot wanted, to separate Rod from his neighbors so that he stood alone.

"You're talking like a kid," Rod said, and turned away.

"Wait." Kane grabbed his arm. "I reckon I am at that."

Rod jerked free, wondering about this. He had never known Kane to come so close to admitting he was wrong about anything. He said, "Sam, when Karl Hermann steps on my toes, I'll fight. Not before."

"Look at it my way," Kane said. "You're young enough to start over, but I'm not, and I've got a wife to think about. If I lose out here, I'll never get another chance."

Kane was an obstinate man with mental capacity for only one idea at a time. Rod had never thought the man was afraid of anything, but he saw that Kane was afraid now, and he began to understand. Most of the nesters had tried somewhere else and failed. Sam Kane was haunted by the fear that Karl Hermann would somehow make him fail again.

"Call off your meeting, Sam," Rod said. "Let's wait till Hermann gets here and see what he does."

"I reckon you're blind because it's your bother who's rodding Spade for Hermann," Kane said bleakly. "Well, I've got just one more thing to say. I've never killed a man in my life, but I'll kill one man or a dozen to hold what little I've got. Egan Valley is about the last place where a man can bring a few head of cows and make a start. Nobody's gonna drive me out."

"Nobody's trying."

"Jason says . . ." Kane stopped, scowling as if he regretted naming Abbot. "We're on the same side, Rod. Don't go over to Hermann."

"Did the notion ever strike you that Abbot's got a game of his own up his sleeve?"

Sullen now, Kane said. "Leave Jason out of this."

"I'm willing if he'll stay out. Tell him that. And tell him that if I ever prove what I suspicion about him, I'll put a window in his ornery, sneaking skull."

Rod walked away, and this time Kane let him go. When Rod reached the timber below the spring, he looked around and saw that Kane was riding back the way he had come. For a moment Rod watched him, his square body hunched forward dejectedly in the saddle.

A keen sense of regret touched Rod. Kane had a following in the valley. Trouble would come regardless of Hermann's intentions, for when a man like Kane was haunted by the fear of persecution as he was, he would not be satisfied until he had the trouble he expected.

Rod followed the small stream that was flowing again, the close-growing pines making a covering overhead and shadowing the trail so that it was nearly dark. The ground sloped sharply here, and when he came out of the pines above his cabin, he saw that the sun was down and twilight was laying a deepening purple hue upon the valley which stretched out for miles below him, the opposite rim blotted from sight by the haze of distance.

Spade's buildings lay twenty miles from here, close to the south shore of Egan Lake and not far from the sand reef which formed the west side of the lake. If that reef ever went out, thousands of acres of lake bottom would be exposed. It might never happen, but if it did, Karl Hermann would have trouble. Kane and his neighbors had talked about it, knowing it would be the best hay land in the valley. They would move onto it, claiming Spade had no right to it, but Hermann was not likely to see it that way.

Hermann had bought Spade from Clay Cummings who had got himself so deeply in debt by picking too many losers on California race tracks that he had been lucky to get anything for his spread. At this moment George Devers would be having supper in the big ranch house, a good supper served by his Chinese cook.

Anger rose in Rod as it invariably did when he thought about his brother who always picked the easy way. Comfortable. Good wages. Give orders to the vaqueros who rode for Spade. Not a worry in the world. Well, it was a good life for George, but it wouldn't do for Rod.

Stepping into the shed behind his cabin, he leaned the shovel against the wall. He slammed the hammer down on the work bench, making a loud clatter. He went out, realizing he wasn't being altogether fair to George who had wanted one thing from life while he had wanted another, for George possessed little of the independent spirit which characterized Rod.

Actually the resentment Rod felt toward George was not due to his choosing security instead of independence. That was a man's privilege. The trouble went back to the time when their father had lost his Nevada ranch to one of Karl Hermann's banks and had died a few months later, frustrated and disappointed.

George had gone to work for Hermann, frankly saying that if you couldn't lick a man, you might just as well throw in with him. That, to Rod, was unforgivable. He'd told George what he thought of him and left the country. After that they had seen each other only at rare intervals, and then usually by accident.

After Rod had settled here in Egan Valley, George had paid him an unexpected visit. He had stayed only a day or two, their talk casual and impersonal, and when he had left, he had ridden south across Spade which at the time had belonged to Clay Cummings.

Within a month Hermann had bought Spade and sent George north to run it. That had been two years ago, and during those two years, Rod had not seen George except on a few Saturday afternoons when they had met on Poplar City's Main Street and exchanged greetings.

Rod came around the corner of the cabin, trying to forget

George and telling himself that as far as Karl Hermann and Spade were concerned, he'd live and let live. All he wanted was to be let alone. Then he saw the horse racked in front of the cabin; he caught the smell of frying ham, and blood began to pound in his temples. Doll Nance had ridden out from town and was cooking supper for him.

Chapter II

Rod STOPPED in the doorway and put a bony shoulder against the jamb. The table was set. Doll stood by the stove, her back to him, unaware that he was there. He stood motionless for a moment, the poignant pleasure that just looking at her gave him beginning to die. He was afraid to ask why she had come.

Doll Nance was twenty, a small girl whose head did not quite come to Rod's shoulder. He had started going with her within a month after he had come to the valley; they had been engaged for a year, and now it seemed to him that he had never known or cared for any other girl.

She was straightforward and direct and he liked that, but she was impetuous and strong-willed, too, and that side of her bothered him. Her sense of humor was crazy and often unpredictable, and there were times when he was uncertain whether she was serious or having fun with him.

Their last date had been a stormy one, for she could not see any connection between their marriage and the fact that Rod owed Jason Abbot two thousand dollars. She had said some biting things about his overgrown pride, and after thinking about them for a week, he still wasn't sure whether she had meant them or not.

He said, "Doll."

She whirled, surprised because she didn't know he was there, then she laughed. "What's the idea, sneaking up on me like a Piute? Who did you think you'd find?"

"Oh, I didn't know. I have a different girl waiting for me every night."

Doll grabbed up a butcher knife and flourished it. "If I ever find another woman with you, I'll scalp her from top to toe." She put the knife down and ran across the room to him. "Rod, it's been such a long week."

She lifted her mouth to be kissed, and when she drew her lips away from his a moment later, he asked, "Satisfactory, Miss Nance?"

"Very satisfactory, Mr. Devers." She put a hand up to his mouth and he kissed the tip of each finger. "I came to tell you that I'll be available for marriage tomorrow at high noon."

So that was why she had come! Looking down at her up-turned face, he sensed the tension that had crept into her. He said lightly, "I'll put it in my date book. I'd better wash up. Looks like supper's about ready."

He walked past her to the bench at the end of the stove, poured water into the wash pan, and scrubbed his face. When he dried and turned toward the table, he saw that Doll was forking ham from the frying pan into a platter.

He sat down at the table, bone-weary. The irritation the day had brought to him began to give way to a sense of well being. It was good to have supper ready when he got in. He thought with keen regret that he could have it this way every evening if he hadn't got himself in debt up to his neck, but it was too late to think about that.

He sat slack in his chair, watching Doll pour the coffee and return to the stove with the pot, walking in the quick, graceful way that was characteristic of her. She took biscuits from the oven, glancing over her shoulder to smile at him.

"I swiped one of Ma's pies," she said. "It'll be good if my cooking isn't."

"What kind?"

"Dried apple." She gave him a conspiratorial wink. "I heard once that the way to a man's heart is through his stomach."

Irritated, he said, "Even if it takes your ma's pies to do the job." Usually he tried to match her light moods, but tonight he was too tired, his temper frayed too thin by the "accidents" that had been plaguing him.

She brought the ham and biscuits to the table and sat down, the smile fading from the corners of her mouth. She wasn't exactly pretty, Rod thought. Her lips were full and red, but too long; her freckle-covered nose was on the pug side. Her auburn hair was loosely pinned at the back of her head, and now that she was close to the lamp, the light made a bright shine on the film of sweat that covered her forehead. But pretty or not, she was his girl and he loved her, and he shouldn't have spoken as he did.

"Let's get along with each other, Rod," she said in a low voice. "For tonight?"

She said it as if it were a question, and he sensed she wasn't quite sure of herself, but she was resolved not to quarrel about their wedding date for the moment at least. He said, "Sure, we'll get along."

She nudged the platter toward him. "I was afraid you were mad at something."

"I am." He helped himself to the ham. "The spring was mudded up again and one side of the fence busted all to hell."

"Oh Rod. Again?" She shook her head, her face warm with sympathy. "Were there any tracks?"

"A horse done it which don't prove nothing. Then to make it worse, Sam Kane rides over and wants to fight Karl Hermann before Hermann ever gets here."

"Oh, I forgot the beans." She jumped up and brought a dish of beans to the table from the warming oven. "What are you going to do?"

"Nothing," he answered. "Not till I get my hands on the gent who's been making my accidents."

Doll sat down again. "Trouble's on the way, Rod. Big trouble. Everybody in town's talking about it. They say Hermann isn't coming to the valley for the ride."

"Aw, they're just jumpy," he said. "We don't have nothing he wants."

But he had something Jason Abbot wanted. Or someone else if he was guessing wrong about Abbot. As he ate, worry began gnawing at his mind again. He thought about Kane's notion that George was responsible for the "accidents," and wondered if he knew his brother as well as he thought he did. A man changed with the years, especially when he worked for a millionaire like Karl Hermann who habitually dominated everything around him.

Doll brought the pie to the table and cut it, glancing at him often, the little, half smile that he knew so well returning to her lips. She was up to something, he thought, and he was afraid to guess what it was. Anything could happen when she was in one of her crazy moods. But she said nothing until he finished his pie.

He leaned back in his chair and rolled a smoke. "Good pie," he said. "Be sure to thank your mother for it."

She rose and ran around the table to him. "I'm not going to let you pretend that pie was the only good thing you had tonight." She took the cigarette from his fingers and laid it on the table, then putting her hands on both sides of his face, kissed him. "Have you got the gall to tell me Ma's pie tasted better than my kiss?"

He pulled her down on his lap and frowned, pretending to give the matter careful thought. Finally he said, "No, I guess your kiss was a little sweeter."

"Must have been a close vote." She put the side of her face against his chest, the top of her head coming under his chin. She whispered, "Tomorrow, Rod. At high noon."

He had no doubt about her mood now. She was completely serious. He was silent, holding her that way for a time. He couldn't say anything without starting a quarrel, and he didn't want to do that. The last quarrel would do for the rest of his life. Suddenly he had the terrifying thought that Doll could not be put off any longer, that she had come out here tonight to make that clear.

In a sudden burst of violence, Doll jerked Rod's arms away from her and jumped up. "How about it, Rod? Will you marry me tomorrow?"

He rose. "Doll, there's nothing I'd rather do, but we can't, with things . . ."

She stiffened, her head canted to one side, listening. She said, "Someone's coming, Rod."

"Probably Kane wanting me to go to that meeting with him."

He walked to the front door and went through it, moving fast. He did not expect any trouble, but he had been in too many range wars to stand silhouetted in a doorway with the light behind him. The rider was close now, a vague shape in the outer darkness. He stopped, still some distance from the hitch pole, and called, "Hello, the house."

Doll, standing just inside the door, said incredulously, "Abbot! What's he doing out here?"

"I can make one guess," Rod said, and raising his voice, called, "Come in, Jason."

Abbot rode on to the hitch pole, dismounted, and tied. He walked up the path, his spurs jingling, and went through the door, Rod following. He was a tall, slender man who called himself a rancher and owned the Flying W, a small spread in the west end of the valley. But in reality ranching was a sideline with him. He spent most of his time in town, buying and selling horses and making loans to the small cowmen, then watching the borrower with frantic concern until the loan was repaid.

Abbot always managed to be the best-dressed man in the valley. He wore a broad-brimmed black hat, a white shirt with a string tie, a Prince Albert, and tight-fitting riding britches.

His boots, invariably polished until they held a high gloss, were imported from California. Abbot liked to brag that they were made by the best boot maker on the Pacific Coast.

"Sit down and have a cup of coffee," Rod said. "Got some pie left."

"No thanks." Abbot's green eyes, as bright and sharp as splintered glass, were fixed on Doll's face. "Looks like I busted into something."

Doll had moved across the room to the stove. She stood with her back to it, her hands clasped behind her. She did not lower her gaze under Abbot's hard scrutiny, and Rod was puzzled by the frank distaste that she showed for Abbot.

A good deal of ugly gossip was bandied about the valley that connected Abbot and Doll's mother. Rod didn't know whether there was anything to it or not, but now it occurred to him that maybe there was and Abbot had come here looking for Doll.

There was this moment of awkward silence, then Rod pulled up a chair for Abbot. "No, you ain't busting into anything. Sit down."

"I'm not of a mind to visit." Reluctantly Abbot turned his gaze from Doll to Rod. "You've heard about Karl Hermann coming to the valley?"

Rod nodded. "Everybody has, I reckon."

"We're scared, Devers," Abbot said. "I'm not ashamed to admit that I am."

"Hermann can't touch you, even if he wanted to."

"You're wrong," Abbot said scornfully, as if he thought Rod was a fool for making such an assertion. "Hermann can touch all of us and he will. You can depend on it he isn't coming here just to inspect Spade."

"Then why is he coming?"

Abbot shook his head as if unable to understand this stupidity. "To take over the valley. I know something of his appetite for land, and I also know he has political connections which will enable him to clean us out of the valley if we don't fight."

"Sam Kane was over today and he was talking the same way," Rod said. "Looks to me like we'd better wait and see what Hermann aims to do."

"I can't afford to wait," Abbot snapped. "I propose to protect my interest and I'll go to any length to do it. That means money, but unfortunately most of my cash is loaned out. I came here tonight to ask you to let me have my two thousand by the end of the week. I'll forget the interest if . . ."

"Let's talk sense," Rod broke in. "The note isn't due for a couple of months."

Abbot's gaze swung to Doll again. He cleared his throat, and with an effort, brought his eyes back to Rod. "Will you guarantee to pick up your note when it's due?"

"You said when I borrowed the money that . . ."

"I know, I know." Abbot made an impatient gesture. "But at the time I had no idea Karl Hermann was coming. I will not be run out of this valley, Devers. If I have to recruit an army to stay, that's what I'll do." He cleared his throat again. "I'll expect that money the first of September."

Rod struggled with his temper, fighting the impulse to drive a fist into Abbot's smug face. He said, "You know I've got some four-year-old steers I was counting on selling to meet your note, but by the time I drive to Winnemucca . . ."

"I don't want excuses," Abbot said crisply. "You will pay the interest and principal on the date the note is due, or I'll take steps."

"You want the heifers?"

Abbot shook his head. "You paid twice what they were worth. I want cash, Devers."

Rod stared at Abbot's cold face that was without the slightest hint of friendly intent. Rod's temper, already pulled thin by the things that had happened the last few hours, suddenly snapped. He started toward Abbot, convinced that the horse trader, for some malicious reason of his own, was determined to smash everything Rod had worked three years to build.

"Rod," Doll cried. "Beating him up won't pay off your note."

"That's right." Abbot had drawn a short-barreled gun from his coat pocket. "Stay where you are, Devers. I didn't come here to fight. As a matter of fact, I'm doing you a favor by letting you know exactly where you stand."

Rod had stopped when Doll called to him. Now he stood a step from Abbot, breathing hard, his eyes on the gun. He said, "I guess you figure stripping my range is doing me a favor. And mudding up my spring and busting my fences are more favors." He motioned to the door. "Git before I take that pop gun away from you and break your damned neck."

"You won't break my neck if I put a hole in your brisket, Devers, but I've said what I came to say, so I'm ready to go." Abbot motioned toward Doll. "I'll take you home."

"You won't take me anywhere, Abbot," the girl breathed.

"I can't leave you out here alone with Devers," Abbot said

harshly. "I think something of your good name even if you don't, and I know what'll happen if . . ."

"Shut up." Rod was white-faced and trembling with the anger that was building up into a wild and uncontrollable fury. "Get out, Abbot, before I kill you."

"I'll go when Doll goes with me." Abbot backed up a step, his green eyes sparked by the hatred he felt for Rod. "If she doesn't, I'll see that everyone in the valley knows she spent the night with . . ."

Doll had grabbed a stove stick from the wood box. Now she started toward Abbot, the stick raised as if she were going to brain him. He swung the gun toward her, yelling, "Drop that."

Rod lunged at him. Abbot jumped back and fired, but his attention had been momentarily diverted and he was slow. The bullet missed Rod by a foot and slapped into the log wall of the cabin, then Rod had him by the right wrist and twisted until the gun fell to the floor. He yanked the man around and kicked him in the seat, sending him plunging headlong through the door to sprawl into the dirt of the yard.

"You open your mug about Doll and I'll blow your teeth through the back of your head," Rod shouted. "You savvy, Abbot?"

The horse trader got to his feet and turned, the lamplight falling across his narrow, bitter face. Rod stood there, waiting, hoping Abbot would make a fight out of this, but that was not his way.

"You're going to find out something you don't know," Abbot said thickly. "I have a good memory."

Abbot swung on his heel and crossed the yard to his horse. He mounted and rode away without another word or a backward glance. Rod stood in the doorway until the sound of hoofs died downslope, then he reached for his gun belt that hung from a peg on the wall. He buckled it around him, and when he looked up, he saw that Doll had dropped into a chair at the table.

"I'm sorry, Rod." She looked at him, her face filled with misery. "He must have got it out of Ma where I was."

Rod stared at her, realizing that she was trying to say Abbot had used the note as an excuse to come here tonight, that it was really Doll's presence which had brought him, but it didn't make sense. Rod knew he had Doll's mother's approval. Whatever purpose the man had was his and his alone.

"It's all right," Rod said. "Abbot didn't do no hurt."

"He will," Doll whispered. "You don't know him. Nobody

knows him but me and Ma. He's the only man I ever met who makes me feel undressed just by looking at me." She stared at the gun on Rod's hip. "Put your gun belt back where it was. It will just make the trouble worse."

Rod knew there was no use to explain to her that it was an old game to him and one he understood, the only difference being that now it was his personal game and always before it had been someone else's. But the signs were the same and he recognized them, the beginning of a pattern that would be woven out of greed and passion and ambition, so it was time to start wearing his gun.

"Maybe," he said. "We've got trouble all right, but it won't be Karl Hermann who'll be responsible for it."

She rose. "Go saddle your sorrel, Rod. I'll clean up the dishes and we'll ride to town."

He left the cabin, thinking about Jason Abbot and wondering what had really prompted his visit. He could only be sure of one thing. There was something back of it he did not understand. Marcia Nance, Doll's mother, might know, but he wasn't sure she would tell him.

When he finished saddling the sorrel, he led the horse to the cabin, wishing he could skip the next hour or two, for he knew what Doll would say. But he could not change his decision about postponing their wedding. Abbot's visit made him more certain than ever that he was right, but Doll would say he was just being stubborn.

Finally it would come to a clash of wills. If he lost her ... He shook his head. Nothing would be worse than that, but for Doll's own good, he could not give in to her. But she'd laugh in his face if he told her that and say she knew better than anyone else what was good for her.

When he went in, she had finished washing and drying the dishes and was putting them away. She glanced over her shoulder at him, smiling briefly. "I hate working in Ma's hotel," she said, "but there's nothing I'd rather do than work for you."

He crossed the room to her and took her hands. He said softly, "Try to understand this, Doll. From the time I was a little kid I've wanted to own a spread. That was why I did things after Dad died that I wasn't proud of, but it was the only way I could make some quick money without robbing a bank or doing something like that."

"I know, Rod." She squeezed his hands. "I can help you. I will, too, if I ever get a chance."

He nodded, wanting her to know he understood how she felt.

"Having supper when I ride in, and well, you just being here is something I want more than anything else. But I'm in trouble, Doll. You saw that tonight. Let's wait to get married until I'm out of debt."

"So we wait and wait and wait." She shook her head, impatient now. "I'm not good at waiting. I love you, Rod. We were going to get married in the spring, and then June. Well, June's about gone."

"We talked it over," he said. "About buying the heifers. It's easy to see now that I was the biggest idiot in Oregon, but I couldn't then. Well, there's no use cussing myself for something that's already done. What I've got to worry about is raising two thousand dollars. When I do, we'll get married."

"I won't quarrel with you again, Rod." She held her head high and proud, her lips quivering. "I'm sorry about the things I said the last time you were in town. Since then, well, I've made up my mind. It's tomorrow or not at all."

She dropped his hands and put her arms around him, the side of her face against his shirt. He said, "Don't say that, Doll. I've seen too many men who got married when they couldn't support their wives. Like Todd Shannon."

"Don't compare yourself to a no-good like Todd Shannon," she cried. "We'll make out."

"Not if we have a family," he said, tight-lipped. "Not even if there's just you and me and Abbot takes my cattle which is about what he's aiming to do. Wait a little longer, Doll. Till fall."

She stepped away from him and walked across the room to where she had hung her hat by the chin strap from a set of antlers. She swung back to face him, jamming her hat on her head. "You know what's wrong, Rod? You've got two loves, the Rocking R and me, and the Rocking R was in your heart a long time before I was."

"It don't mean I love you any less because . . ."

"I won't come second to a ranch, Rod. I'm first, or I'm nothing."

"Oh hell," he said, exasperated now. "You and the Rocking R are two different things. A man don't love his wife like he does his ranch."

"Yes, we're different things," she said brightly. "I'd cook for you and patch your clothes and clean your cabin. I'd sleep with you and keep you warm and give you pleasure. Not like Ma and Abbot . . ."

She whirled and ran outside. So the gossip was true, Rod

thought. He blew out the lamp and closed the door, and when he reached the hitch rail, Doll was already in the saddle.

"I shouldn't have said that," she whispered. "It's just that I'm haunted by the feeling that if we got married, we'd be happy, but if we wait, we'll lose our chance. I'm afraid of Abbot, Rod, I'm terribly afraid."

Looking up at her face, a faint oval in the starshine, he sensed that she was giving him this last chance. Still, he could not change. She had no reason to be afraid of Abbot; she was in no danger from him. What he and her mother did was their business. If Rod got out of debt by fall, he and Doll could be married, but if he didn't, she was better off without him. It was that simple if he could make her see it.

"When a man has any pride, Doll," he said slowly, "he wants to take care of his wife because he loves her, but if he's broke . . ."

"Pride." She screamed the word at him, her pent-up feelings breaking through her self-control. "If you say that word one more time, I'll . . . I'll . . ."

She didn't finish. She wheeled her horse and started down-slope toward town. Rod stepped into the saddle and caught up with her. They hadn't quarreled this time, not the way they had before, but they were finished. Perhaps it was better to cut it off with one quick stroke than to keep gnawing at it and making themselves unhappy.

He looked up at the sky, the stars glittering like cold, brilliant jewels, and he knew he was trapped. He was wrong if he married Doll tomorrow; if he didn't, he lost her. Then a strange and startling thought struck him. He wondered if God knew the answers, and if He did, how did He pass the word along?

Chapter III

MARCIA NANCE usually gave Doll the evening stint behind the desk, but tonight Marcia was forced to take the desk herself. She hadn't wanted Doll to ride out to the Rocking R, but Doll was twenty, a grown woman, and the day was gone when she could order Doll's life for her. So she made no objection when Doll had told her where she was going.

Marcia helped Ada Larkin in the dining room during the rush hour, keeping an eye on the lobby. As soon as the dining room was empty, she brought the pillow case she was embroidering from her parlor in the rear of the building and perched herself on the stool behind the desk.

Tonight she found no interest in the embroidery. She laid the pillow case on the register beside her scissors, and plucking the thimble from her finger tip, placed it beside the needle on the cloth that had been drawn tight inside the double hoop. She had been working on the pillow case for Doll's bed for weeks, but she wasn't getting anything done. It was always this way, her nerves drawn so taut that she felt like screaming.

Marcia had learned long ago that men did not like nervous women, especially screaming ones. She wasn't sure she understood women, not even Ada Larkin who helped in the kitchen and dining room, although there was nothing complex about Ada who worked because she had to help support her father and mother and the steadily increasing brood of children that filled the Larkin cabin.

Marcia wasn't sure she understood Doll, either. She wasn't sure she understood herself. Now, mentally honest, she realized that was the cause of her trouble. She had started something with Jason Abbot that she could not stop, but when it had begun, she had not known how tragic a mistake she was making.

She did understand men, for she had lived in a man's world almost as long as she could remember. If she hadn't known how to get along with them, she could not have survived. The trou-

18

ble was Jason Abbot was no ordinary man. He was a little crazy. She was to blame for that, too.

The evening had been a quiet one, but now a man had ridden into town and tied at the hitch pole in front of the hotel. Marcia slid off the stool and stood waiting behind the desk, hoping it wasn't Abbot and yet terribly afraid it was. Then, relieved, she saw that it was Pablo Sanchez, George Devers' segundo.

Sanchez removed his sombrero and bowed. He was a good-looking man, tall and slender, and probably the best vaquero in the valley. He said, "Good evening, *Senora*."

She said, "Good evening," and puzzled over why he was here. Spade men seldom came to town, and when they did, they never stopped at the hotel.

"I am looking for *Senor* Rod Devers," Sanchez said. "Is he in town?"

"No." Marcia hesitated, her curiosity stirred. She did not know what the barrier was that lay between Rod and his brother, but she sensed that the barrier was there. Now it seemed inconceivable that George would have sent his segundo to Poplar City to find Rod. "What do you want him for?"

"I do not know," Sanchez said, smiling blandly.

"I deserved that." She laughed, knowing she had been nosey. Men didn't like nosey women any better than they liked nervous ones, but it didn't matter with Sanchez. "I think he'll be in later this evening, but I don't have any idea when."

"I will wait," he said.

"If he comes in, I'll tell him you want to see him."

"*Muchas gracias*," Sanchez said, and turning, walked into the bar.

She watched him until he disappeared, a vague uneasiness in her. Then she told herself that if anyone could take care of himself, it was Rod Devers. She could think of several reasons why Rod would make a good husband for Doll, and that was one.

She knew Rod's background and she had seen what he had done with the Rocking R. Whatever happened, he was the kind of man who would take care of his wife. Somehow she had to get them married before Karl Hermann's coming blew up the keg of powder that she and Jason Abbot had so carefully placed here in the valley.

She reached for her embroidery and let her hand drop back into her lap. Alone, she permitted her thoughts to run down the bitter channel they had taken so often these last weeks. She

loved Doll so much that it had become an obsession, a posses-
sive love that crowded everything out of her heart except her
hatred for Karl Hermann. Now she saw that what she had done
would hurt Doll.

Marcia felt as if she had dug out a spring and brought a tor-
rent down upon her that was sweeping her to destruction. Doll,
too, because Doll loved Rod Devers. She remembered how Doll
had played with dominoes when she had been little, setting
them on end in a long row and then tipping the last one over. It
knocked down the one next to it and on along the line until all
of them were flat.

Doll had played that way an hour at a time, a childish game
that had given her pleasure, but it wasn't childish the way
Marcia was playing it. She had not realized how one event
would lead to another until her scheming for revenge against
Karl Hermann had woven a web that had trapped Rod.

There must be some escape from the trap she had set, but
she had thought about it for days, and only one possible solution
had come to her. If Rod would marry Doll and take her away,
they would be all right. But Rod was a proud and stubborn man.
He would not ask for help; he would not take it if it were offered. She had to try, but she knew she would fail.

Some of the trouble lay in Doll who simply could not understand that a man like Rod was not to be hurried. Marcia folded
her hands and squeezed them together, her knuckles white with
the pressure. Doll had made a mistake going out to Rod's place
tonight. Marcia knew what Doll would say and do in her impetuous way, and Rod would get stubborn.

Things had not been right between them for weeks, although
it had not been long ago when their marriage had been taken
for granted by everyone who knew them. Rod had made a mistake borrowing from Abbot, a mistake Marcia had been unable
to prevent, so he was in financial trouble, and while she could
see Rod's viewpoint, she knew that Doll couldn't. Or wouldn't.
She wanted to get married now and she could see no reason
for waiting if they loved each other. It was that simple to her.

Suddenly Marcia was afraid, terribly afraid of what Doll
would tell her when she got back to town. Doll would try to push
Rod and Rod wouldn't be pushed. It would be the end, she
thought, and she didn't know what would happen to Doll. There
was the other side, too. If Rod did marry Doll and take her
away, Marcia would never see her again.

Loving Doll as she did, she knew there would be nothing left
for her. Too great a price to pay for revenge on Karl Hermann,

far too great. She could see the dominoes falling in front of her, falling, falling, until they were all down.

A sob wrenched her body. She stood up and gripped the edge of the desk, her head bowed, and she wondered if she could find the strength she would need to kill Jason Abbot. But it was probably too late for any remedy, even one as drastic as that.

A door slammed in the back of the hotel and she heard Abbot's querulous voice, "Marcia."

She fought her weakness for a moment, not wanting him to know. She didn't want to see him, but there was no way to avoid it. She called, "What is it, Jason?"

"Come back here to the parlor," he ordered.

"Just a minute," she said, and stepping into the dining room, called, "Ada, watch the desk."

She returned to the lobby, and picking up her embroidery, walked down the hall to her parlor. It was her room, the one place in the hotel which was really hers. Here she could read or sew or just be alone with her thoughts. Somehow it never seemed right for Abbot to come here, but he came often enough and she should be used to it.

He slammed the door behind her the instant she stepped into the room. She saw at once that he was angry and hurt and in a vicious mood. He was dirty, too, and that was unusual. Neatness was a fetish with him.

"What happened, Jason?" she asked.

"I went out to the Rocking R to get Doll," he said thickly. "Devers got the drop on me and threw me out." He swallowed. "Kicked me through the door." He swallowed again. "I'll kill him, Marcia. God damn him, I'll kill him."

She gripped his arm. "Jason, you're out of your mind. You said you'd get him out of the country. You said he wouldn't be harmed. You promised."

He jerked his arm free and began pacing the floor. "I've done all I could to get him to leave, but he won't go. Sam Kane went to see him tonight, but he won't come to the meeting. That puts him on Hermann's side. Can't you see what that means, a gunslinger with his reputation?"

"He won't go over to Hermann," she said quickly. "He hates Hermann, too. You haven't handled him right. I told you . . ."

"Sure, sure," he jeered. "Use honey instead of vinegar, you said. Hell, that wouldn't work with him. He's got a one-track mind. The only thing he wants is to own his spread. He's said it a dozen times. When he borrowed that money, I thought . . ." Abbot paused, a muscle in his cheek started to jerk. "That won't work, either. He'll bull it through, and by the time his note's due, it'll be too late."

He began to pace the floor again. Marcia dropped her embroidery on the oak table in the center of the room and sat down in her rocking chair. She watched Abbot, thinking what a small-souled man he was, goaded by an ambition that was far too great for his talents. That was why he had gone crazy, she thought, reaching for something which was beyond him. She was to blame for that, too, because she had known from the first what she could do with him.

"You could be as big as Karl Hermann," she had told him over and over. "You just haven't had the chance, but if you owned Spade and if you could control the rest of the valley, you would be the biggest man in this corner of the state."

She had fed his ego that way for months, and he had believed her because he wanted to believe her. Now he would say she was lying, even if she told him the truth. She had never loved him as she had said, but she had used him, fanning the spark of self-importance that had always been in him into a roaring flame.

She said nothing while he kept on pacing. She knew that his injured pride would never let him make any sort of a deal with Rod; he would never forgive him for kicking him through the door. He had hired Todd Shannon to do the little, dirty things he wanted done, the spying on Rod and George Devers and even Sam Kane; he had imported Chuck England and Barney Webb, killers who would do exactly what he wanted. Because of them he had become a dangerous man.

Marcia had found him a small rancher, a horse trader with a little money and burdened by an exaggerated ego; she had changed him into a scheming murderer because she had seen in him a tool she could use against Karl Hermann. She had started on him the day she had heard Hermann had bought Spade, knowing that sooner or later Hermann would come to Egan Valley.

Now that it was too late she condemned herself. She began to rock furiously, realizing how futile regrets were. She tried desperately to think of some way out of this, some escape that would at least save Rod. Because she could think of nothing, she suddenly rose and moved around the table to block Abbot's path.

"Jason," she said coldly, "I wanted Rod out of the country because Doll loves him and he will make a good husband for her. I don't want either of them hurt. Do you understand that?"

He stopped, green eyes fixed on her strained face. "I'm not playing this game to give you what you want. I won't permit Doll to marry Devers. I love her, too, you know."

She had never heard him say that before, and for a moment she didn't understand. She said, "I'm her mother . . ." Then she stopped. Not once had Abbot ever mentioned marrying her. Now she understood a number of things: the little courtesies he had shown Doll, the presents he had given her, the sly methods he had used to be alone with her. And all the time she had thought he only wanted Doll to accept him as a stepfather.

She laughed hysterically. Abbot had been using her, too. She cried, "You poor fool! Do you know what Doll thinks of you?"

"It isn't important what she thinks of me now," Abbot said harshly. "All I want to do is to keep her from marrying Devers. When I get to where I'm going, she'll come to me. Money and position are two things no woman can refuse." He tapped his chest. "I'm Jason Abbot. I'll be a greater man than Karl Hermann ever was. You've said so yourself."

"And I'm a fool, too," she breathed, "or I never would have said it. Let Hermann come and let him go. A lot of people are going to be hurt. It isn't worth it." She gripped both of his arms, her hands biting into his flesh with savage intensity. "I've been wrong, Jason. All I really want is for Doll to be happy."

"I'll see to that." He stepped back, jerking free from her grip. "You are a fool to think I'd drop this now. I don't need you any more. I don't even know why I came here tonight."

But she knew. When things went wrong, he always came to her and she told him what a great man he was. He wanted that assurance now, but she would not give it to him. Suddenly it came to her that if she could make him see himself, really see himself, this whole thing could be stopped.

"I've lied to you, Jason," she whispered. "I'm sorry, but you'll never be a great man. I told you that because I wanted to hurt Karl Hermann, and I thought . . ."

"So you think you lied to me? Well, you didn't. I'll be the biggest man . . ."

"Jason, Jason, can't you understand? You're little and you'll always be little. No one ever makes a silk purse out of a pig's ear."

His thin face was white. He opened his mouth and closed it: he licked his lips with the tip of his tongue, and then his control broke and he was an animal of fury. He stepped toward her and hit her on the side of her face, rocking her head with the blow. He wheeled to the door; he opened it and then looked back.

"There are some things Doll doesn't know about you. If you don't want me to tell her, be careful what you say about me."

He left the room then, moving in the jerky way of a man whose nerves are so taut they are ready to snap. She lunged to her table and pulled a drawer open; she picked up the gun she kept there, then his steps died and the back door slammed shut. Too late! She felt of her face where he had struck her and blinked back the tears.

Men were riding into town. Kane and Otto Larkin and the others. They would have their meeting. They would talk about what to do when Hermann reached the valley. And Rod . . . She laid the gun back and pushed the drawer shut. She had to see Rod when he got here; she had to be composed when she talked to him.

Slowly she walked down the hall to the lobby, leaving the lamp burning on the oak table. She had always considered herself a hard-headed, practical woman, refusing to give way to sentiment when it stood in her way. Now she realized it had been a pose, an emotional hideout.

A long time ago she had been hurt because she had loved Karl Hermann, and because of that love, her entire life had been twisted and warped. Now she must think of Doll. She stood behind her desk, only vaguely aware of the activity in the street, for she was planning what she would say to Rod.

Chapter IV

NEITHER Rod nor Doll felt like talking as they left the Rocking R. Rod's thoughts were a sour stream. He tried to focus his mind on Jason Abbot, tried to figure out why Abbot was so determined to break him. He could find no satisfactory answer, but at least the man had come into the open.

Only a miracle could prevent three years of hard work and hope from being lost. Rod was not sure he could start over. He had seen men broken by hard luck until they were no good to themselves or anyone else. The realization that he had only himself to blame did not help. He had got into debt simply because he had been in too big a hurry to get where he wanted to be. What had looked like a good gamble last spring had turned out to be a bad one. But Doll would be his big loss, not the Rocking R.

He glanced at her, realizing that no matter how hard he tried to put her out of his mind, his thought cycle always returned to her. What had been a mere boyhood ambition had taken on real meaning because of Doll. But she wouldn't or couldn't understand that. Resentment rose in him then. If she was breaking it off because she wasn't getting her way, he didn't want her for a wife. But he was rationalizing, finding excuses for himself, and it didn't help.

The country tipped down for three miles below Rod's cabin, then leveled off. The road followed Egan Creek. Once it had finished its brawling passage out of the Blue Mountains, it became a slowly moving stream, meandering across the valley to flow into Egan Lake another five miles beyond Poplar City.

Now, with the lights of the town directly before them, Rod said, "Thanks for coming out and cooking supper."

"You're welcome," Doll said crisply.

He was silent until they reached the first outlying houses of the town, lamplight bright in their windows, and then he broke down his pride enough to say, "You busted it off, Doll, but maybe it'll make you feel good to know I'll always love you. There'll never be anyone else."

She laughed shortly. "Not till the next time a wind lifts some skirt enough for you to see a pretty ankle, if there are any pretty ankles in Egan Valley besides mine."

She was breaking it off, clean and sharp, and she was working herself into a rage so she could do it right. He was angry then, and when they reached the hotel, he said, "Tell your ma I'll need a room tonight, but don't think I'm staying on the chance of seeing you again."

"That's just fine because I never want to see you again as long as I live." Doll dismounted and handed the reins to Rod. "Put my horse up."

He hesitated, hating her at that moment, and then he thought how silly this was. You didn't really love a woman if you got so angry you thought you hated her, so he didn't hate her and he never would. "Sure, I'll take care of him."

She looked up at him, standing so that the light from the hotel touched the side of her face. He saw the hurt and the misery that was so clearly shown there, and wondered what she was seeing in his face.

She must have realized she was letting him see her feelings. She cried, "Go poke your face in a horse trough," and whirled and ran into the lobby.

He rode on down the street to the livery stable, leading Doll's horse. When he came back through the archway a moment later, he considered going into the Palace. The best thing that could happen to him would be to get into a hell of a good fight.

What kind of a fool woman was it anyhow who broke things off because he wouldn't marry her tomorrow? Chances were he couldn't rig up a fight just now when he wanted one. Well, he'd get drunk, so drunk they'd heave him into the alley and he couldn't think about Doll for a week. But it wouldn't do any good because he'd start thinking about her when the week was over.

A long line of horses stood racked in front of the saloon, and when he saw them, he remembered Sam Kane's meeting. He shrugged and moved along the walk to the hotel. To hell with the meeting! Feeling the way he did now, he might get his fight and wind up killing the wrong man. Better stay out of it, he decided, and stepped into the hotel lobby.

He crossed to the desk, feeling the stagnant heat that the room still harbored from the warm day. He touched the brim of his hat, saying, "Howdy," to Marcia who was behind the desk.

"Good evening, Rod." She had a special tone of voice for him that he had never heard her use on any other man, one way she had of letting him know she favored him for a son-in-law. "Doll said you'd be in. You can have Room 12. It's on the front corner and it'll be cooler than the others."

He said, "Thanks," and waited for her to give him the key.

But she was in no hurry. She stood with her hands on the desk, blue eyes on him in a searching look that seemed to probe his mind. He knew, then, that Doll had told her mother what had happened.

"How does it feel to have a girl want to marry you tomorrow and you have to turn her down?" Marcia asked.

"Like hell. I forgot to fetch your pie pan back."

He didn't want to discuss Doll. He shifted his weight uneasily, not knowing what to expect. He liked and respected Marcia. When he had come to the valley, she had just started operating the hotel, and the talk was that Jason Abbot had put up most of the money. Those who were inclined to gossip made a good deal out of it. From what Doll had said tonight, it was probably true, but it didn't make Rod think any the less of her.

She was surprisingly young to have a grown daughter, and she was handsome in a mature way that Doll had not yet achieved. Her hair was darker than Doll's, although in the light of the bracket lamp above her, it seemed definitely red. There was a close resemblance between Doll and her mother, and now, meeting Marcia's gaze, Rod was more aware of it than ever. In another fifteen years, he thought, Doll would look exactly as Marcia looked now.

"Have you got time to talk, Rod?" Marcia asked.

He looked away, frowning, then he said, "Sure."

"We'll go back into the parlor," she said, "but you'd better step into the bar first. Pablo Sanchez rode into town about an hour ago. He was looking for you, and I told him I thought you'd be in town later tonight."

"I don't want to see Pablo."

She shrugged. "I'll tell him, but I'll slowly die of curiosity, wondering what he wanted."

Sanchez had worked for Karl Hermann since he'd been a boy. He had come north with George Devers when Hermann had sent George to Spade. Most of the old crew had stayed on, several of them Mexican vaqueros who had come with Clay Cummings when he had driven his first herd to the valley, and after Cummings had sold out, he had asked Hermann to keep the crew. Rod did not know Sanchez well, but he had heard that he was a capable man and that the buckaroos who had worked for Cummings liked and respected him.

Then Rod remembered what Sam Kane had said about George being back of the "accidents" which had pestered him for so long, and he wondered if there could be some connection between those "accidents" and Sanchez' presence in town.

Marcia had started toward the bar. Rod caught up with her, saying, "I'll see what he wants," and went on through the door that opened into the bar.

Sanchez was playing solitaire at one of the poker tables, his sombrero on the other side of the cards. When he saw Rod, he picked up his sombrero and rose, a quick smile making a flash of white against the swarthy background of his skin.

"Mrs. Nance, she say you might be along, *amigo*," Sanchez said, "so I wait."

"She said you wanted to see me."

Sanchez nodded, still smiling. "The boss wants you to come to Spade."

"Nothing to keep George from riding this way," Rod said brusquely.

Sanchez spread his hands. "But already the smell of trouble, she is in the air. *Senor* Devers, he say he might start it if he rode into town, so it would be better if you came to Spade."

"What kind of trouble?"

Sanchez shrugged. "*Quién sabe?* She is in the air like a bad stink in your nose. We do not want it, *amigo,* but she is there."

"I've got plenty of trouble without taking on some of Spade's."

"But we are all together. *Senor* Devers, he say his brother can help."

The impulse was in Rod to say no and walk out, but he hesitated, considering this request which was so utterly unexpected. He had never known George to ask for help from anyone, to ask it from his brother was so fantastic it was unbelievable. Sanchez probably knew what George had in mind, but Rod was sure the vaquero would say nothing more.

Because his curiosity was stirred, Rod said, "I'll be out in the morning."

Sanchez nodded, smiling again. "*Bueno.*"

Returning to the lobby, Rod saw that Marcia was not behind the desk. As he hesitated, Doll came out of the dining room. She said with cool indifference, "Why don't you go to bed?"

Rod had learned a long time ago that Doll's mood could swing from one extreme to the other in a short space of time. She appeared utterly composed, and now, standing a few feet from her, it seemed to Rod that they were complete strangers.

Matching her cool tone, he said, "Your ma wanted to talk."

"Nothing to talk about." He saw the familiar sparkle of deviltry in her eyes as she added, "Go on to bed. Maybe by morning you'll get around to thinking what it would be like if I was in bed with you."

He made his lips form a smile, hoping she would think he was taking this as lightly as she was. He said, "Now maybe I will," and turning, walked rapidly down the hall to Marcia's parlor in the back of the building. The door was open and he saw that Marcia was sitting in her rocking chair, a pillow case that she was embroidering on her lap.

"Come in, Rod," she said.

He stepped into the room and closed the door. "George sent for me." He dropped into a leather chair on the other side of the oak table. "I'm going out to Spade in the morning."

She glanced at him. "What does your brother want?"

He sensed a wariness in her that seemed out of place. He said, "Sanchez didn't say." There was a moment of awkward silence while he rolled a smoke, then he asked, "How did you know I'd be in town tonight?"

"I knew Doll had gone to see you. You wouldn't let her ride back by herself." Marcia glanced at him again, letting him see the worry and concern that was in her. "Doll told me what happened. You're a strong-willed man, Rod. Sometimes you're filled with so much stubbornness and pride that there doesn't seem to be room in you for anything else."

He hadn't come to hear Marcia discuss his faults. He reached for a match, saying, "Did you ever think that Doll might have the same trouble?"

She nodded, her hands idle now on the pillow case. "I have thought of it many times, Rod. In some ways you're an awfully lot alike."

"And did it ever occur to you that I love her so much I won't marry her while I'm up to my neck in debt?" he asked.

"Yes, I've thought of that." She pointed to the gun on his hip. "Doll said Jason had been out there, but why . . ."

"If she told you about Abbot, you know why I'm wearing it."

"Yes, I . . . I suppose I know." She folded her hands and

rocked steadily for a moment, the only sound in the room the squeak of the chair under her. Then she asked, "Rod, what is it you want more than anything else in the world?"

"My own outfit. I've wanted it since I was a kid. After Hermann's bank took our spread, I knew I had to do it alone. That's why I'm in this jam, starting without enough capital and borrowing from Abbot."

"Then Doll was right," Marcia said in a low voice. "The Rocking R is your first love. I'm sorry, Rod."

He struck a match and lighted his cigarette, angry because she had trapped him into saying something that wasn't exactly true. He said, "No, that's wrong. Owning my outfit is twice as important as it used to be because I want to be able to take care of her. I won't marry her till I can."

"I see." Marcia continued to rock, the pulse beat in her temple a steady throbbing. "Rod, I know you've heard the gossip about me and Jason. I won't deny it. I won't even defend myself except to say that I haven't had an easy life. Doll was born when I was sixteen. Since then there have been times when I wasn't sure she'd have anything to eat from one meal to the next, and times when I didn't."

"You don't have to tell me . . ."

"I want you to hear this, Rod. I was hurt once, hurt so deeply that I haven't thought of much except revenge since then. I know that was wrong, and I also know that the only good thing about me is my love for Doll. I want the best for her, so I'd like to help you because she loves you. I have some influence with Jason. I'll talk to him if you'll let me. About your note."

"I've never got behind a woman's skirt. I won't now."

"You are stubborn," she said. "I'm sorry. I thought it was one way I could avert the trouble that's coming."

"What do you know about the trouble that's coming?"

She rose and walked to the window and stood there, a hand gripping the chintz curtain, her body rigid. "I know all about it. I hate Jason. I hate myself. It's like a bog. You take one wrong step and it sucks you in."

Rod rose. "No need to hurt yourself talking . . ."

"Wait. I've got to tell you." She turned to him, her face so pale that he was afraid she was going to faint. "Jason is, well, sort of crazy. I've seen him walk around this room for half an hour at a time, snapping his fingers and hitting himself on the chest and shouting that the day will come when he'll be a bigger man than Karl Hermann. That's what's back of this talk of trouble. He has money, quite a bit, and in a roundabout way he's done all he can to stir up a fight."

"He must be crazy to think he can lick Hermann."

"Possessed is a better word, possessed by an evil spirit. He knows how Hermann got his start, how everything he touched turned to money, and he said he can do the same once he begins to grow. If Hermann was killed, his property would go to his daughter, and Jason believes he could buy Spade for a song if that happened."

"He wouldn't murder Hermann."

"Yes he would." Marcia threw out her hands in a gesture of helplessness. "No one can stop him. He's worked hard to build up fear in Kane and the rest of them. It's made them crazy, too. You can do that with fear, you know, if you're sly and clever like Jason."

He found this hard to believe, for he had never thought of Jason Abbot as anything but a horse trader and a small rancher with a little money which he loaned out at a high rate of interest.

"Why is he putting the screws on me?" Rod asked.

She looked away, biting her lower lip. "He's afraid of you because you're the one man in the valley he can't control. You may be able to turn the others against him. He's spent hours talking about Hermann's cruelty and greed, and he keeps reminding Kane and the rest that George is Hermann's man. You're George's brother. That makes you Jason's enemy." She hesitated, then added, "Now you're going out to Spade. Jason will say that proves it."

"So Abbot's been causing my bad luck?"

She nodded. "He knows that you can be beaten by constant pressure, but not by any direct threat he could make."

She walked back to her rocking chair and sat down. Rod, watching her, realized that worry had brought her close to the breaking point and that it was Doll's future which bothered her.

"You can't change Abbot's mind about collecting that note, can you?" he asked.

"No, but I might be able to persuade him to make you a fair offer for your cattle if you would leave the country."

"I couldn't take it."

"No, I suppose you're too bullheaded." She took a long breath. "You're still young, Rod. There's one thing you haven't learned. A man can't live alone. Jason will see to it that you lose every friend you have in the valley. What will you do then?"

"Put a slug into Abbot's head."

"And Sam Kane and his bunch will lynch you." She hesitated, and then as Rod moved to the door, she said, "Please don't tell anyone what I said about Jason."

He paused, one hand on the knob, his eyes on her bleak face. There was bitterness in her he had never sensed before, and it surprised him, for he had always found her a pleasant woman, given to joking and easy laughter, but tonight she had let him have a glimpse of her tortured soul.

"I'm not a blabber mouth," he said.

"I know you're not," she said quickly. As he opened the door, she cried, "If you love Doll, marry her and take her away from here. Anywhere. I'll stake you to a start somewhere else. Please, Rod."

"I can't do it," he said, and left the room.

When he went through the lobby, he saw with relief that Doll was not behind the desk. He wondered if she'd had anything to do with what Marcia had just said. He paused outside on the walk and smoked a cigarette, thinking that whatever trouble was coming would not affect Doll. Why, then, had Marcia been so anxious to get him out of the valley?

He threw his cigarette away in a sudden, violent gesture, finding no answer to the question, and crossed the street to the Palace. He would be perfectly happy, he thought gloomily, if there were no women in the world.

Chapter V

Rod's only purpose in going into the saloon was to find out what had come of Kane's meeting. As he pushed through the batwings, he saw the men at the bar turn and look at him and then give him their backs, all but old Clay Cummings who stood at one end of the bar, and he remembered Marcia Nance saying, "Jason will see to it that you lose every friend you have in the valley."

In that one moment he glimpsed the dark and barren expression on the faces of his neighbors, their hostility flowing toward him like a blast of foul air. These were men he had known for three years; he had ridden roundup with them spring and fall and once a year had helped drive a pool herd to the railroad at Winnemucca.

Only Clay Cummings stood alone at the bar, a craggy-faced, white-headed eagle of a man. Rod walked to him, motioning to the bartender who brought a bottle and a glass. Rod said, "Howdy, Clay. How are you?"

"If you're asking about my health," the old man said, "I'll tell you it ain't good. Ever see a nightmare, Rod? I mean, see it start little and grow big until it looks like a pink cow twenty feet tall, the kind you see when you're drunk?"

"No," Rod answered. "Have a drink with me, Clay?"

Cummings said, "Why not? We might as well see a few pink cows."

"Not today," Rod said. "This ain't the time."

Cummings shrugged his bony shoulders. "Dunno 'bout that. One time looks as good as another to me."

Rod filled the glasses and they lifted them and drank. Cummings ran the back of a hairy hand across his mouth, and putting his hand on the bar again, began nudging the shot glass back and forth between thumb and forefinger. He had been the first real settler in the valley, coming in the late sixties when the Piutes were a constant menace and the only other whites within fifty miles were the soldiers at Camp Harney.

Cummings had settled between the lakes on Halfmile Creek; he had built a big white house and furnished it extravagantly. He had bought fifty thousand acres of swamp land from the state; he had claimed all the valley and seventy miles of grassland to the south along the Steens Mountains.

At one time Cummings had been worth half a million, then his luck had turned sour, largely because he couldn't keep from going to California every summer and betting on horse races. Once he got behind, he had not been able to come back, so he had borrowed repeatedly from the banks. Finally he had been forced to sell to Karl Hermann, salvaging nothing from his empire but a small ranch on the east side of the Steens fifty miles to the south.

Cummings said, "You ain't real popular with this crowd, Devers. Sam Kane separated the sheep from the goats tonight, and you're a goat."

"No place in between, I reckon," Rod said.

"Not for them that's in the valley. Funny thing the way men get boogered till they run like a stampeding herd of steers. They'll go right over a rim once they get going. I recollect once a storm started a herd of mine to stampeding and I lost every damn head."

"Anybody trying to turn these boys?"

"Wouldn't be no use. I've been standing here listening to Sam tonight. Loco, just plain loco. Shoot Hermann on sight, he says. Otherwise they'll get cleaned out. You don't get big like he done and be honest, Sam says. Only difference between Hermann and a common rustler is size."

"He's partly right," Rod said. "Just partly."

Cummings stroked his white beard, faded blue eyes fixed on Rod's face. "Not even partly, sonny. Hermann is smart and he never misses a chance to make a dollar, but that ain't the same as being crooked."

Rod didn't argue. He'd heard George say the same thing about Hermann, and now he began to wonder if he had been wrong all these years and George had been right. It was not a pleasant thought. He stared down at the shiny surface of the cherrywood bar, unaware that Todd Shannon had come to stand beside him until the man said, "You should have been here tonight, Devers."

Startled, Rod glanced up. Shannon was his neighbor to the west, a furtive, lazy man who neglected his wife and children and lost more cattle every winter than any other rancher in the valley. Still, he always had money for poker or whiskey. It was a puzzle that no one had been able to explain.

"Reckon you were here with bells on, Todd," Rod said.

"You're damned right. What Sam says makes sense. We hit first or we're licked. Hermann's got a bunch of outlaws on Spade, and when he gets here, he'll run us over the hill. He's done it on every range wherever he got a toe hold."

"Sounds like Sam," Rod said.

"Talk," Cummings snorted. "Just fool talk. Why, them boys on Spade worked for me. Most of 'em, anyhow. Ain't an outlaw in the bunch."

Shannon blew out a long breath, the tips of his sweeping mustache quivering. "Easy enough for you to say, Clay, living where you do and being a bachelor, but most of us have wives and kids, and by hell, we'll fight for 'em."

"Ever try working for 'em?" Cummings asked truculently.

"You on Hermann's side?" Shannon demanded.

"I ain't on nobody's side," the old man snapped. "I just want to get along, but this crazy business tonight ain't gonna do nobody no good."

"Abbot here?" Rod asked.

"Got in for the tail end of the meeting," Shannon said. "Didn't have much to say. He's in the back room now with Sam. Chuck England and Barney Webb are with 'em." He cleared his throat, giving Rod a characteristic, sidelong glance. "Was I you, Devers, I'd dust along."

"I ain't quite ready," Rod said irritably.

"Just thought I'd tell you," Shannon muttered, and walked away.

"Damned old woman," Cummings said. "Never did like a man who could walk up on you without being heard."

"Just what did they do tonight?"

"Organized what they're calling the 99," Cummings said. "Sam's the head of it. Him and Abbot and that beanpole of an Otto Larkin are what they call an executive committee."

"They decide anything?"

"They gave this here committee power to decide things." Cummings shook his head. "I'm out of it, being so far south, but it's bad business. Murdering Karl Hermann won't fetch 'em nothing but trouble."

The door of the back room was flung open and Jason Abbot walked out. Sam Kane followed, then Rod saw England and Webb, Abbot's men who worked on his ranch and handled the horses that he traded for. Both were wearing guns. Rod was startled, for it was the first time since he had come to the valley that he had seen a man carry a gun except an occasional drifter who had been riding through the country.

The four men paused, then Abbot saw Rod, and walked toward him, his narrow, wolfish face more flushed than usual. The other three remained in the rear of the room, but Todd Shannon and Otto Larkin and the others who had been standing at the bar now swung in behind Abbot, forming a solid line as they tacitly accepted his leadership. Then Kane left England and Webb, and pushing through the crowd, stopped beside Larkin.

"I understand Sam told you how it was this afternoon and asked you to come to the meeting." Abbot faced Rod, standing not more than ten feet from him. His voice had a ring of authority as if he felt a current of power generated by the knowledge that he had the backing of the crowd behind him. "You didn't come to the meeting, Devers."

"Why, I guess I didn't," Rod said mildly.

"We're organized now," Abbot said, a sense of his importance weighing heavily upon him. "We will see to it that Hermann hears as soon as he gets to the valley."

"I reckon that'll scare him right back over the pass," Rod murmured.

"You won't get anywhere talking smart." Abbot stood very straight, wearing his dignity with the same ease that he wore his fine clothes. "You're taking a stand, Devers." He motioned to the men behind him. "It's only fair that you tell us exactly where you stand. Sam says you made it clear to him you won't have anything to do with us."

Now that it was too late, Rod realized he had made a mistake coming here tonight, that he had played into Abbot's hands. But he couldn't back up. If Abbot was calling for a showdown, this was as good a time as any. Rod glanced at the men behind Abbot, then at Webb and England who were standing like two watch dogs in the rear of the room, and brought his eyes back to Abbot.

"That ain't what I said, but I'll sure as hell tell you what I think." Rod hesitated, wondering if this was what Abbot had meant when he'd said he had a good memory, then he added, "You and Sam and anybody else who kicks up a lot of dust before we know what we're up against is a damned fool and I don't want any part of it."

Abbot swung around to look at Kane and Larkin and the

others. "You heard him, gentlemen." He wheeled back to Rod. "You stand alone, Devers. The rest of us propose to defend what is ours. It would be suicide to allow a man to remain among us who is frankly a traitor."

"By God, I'm not the traitor," Rod shouted. "It's you."

"Me." Abbot threw up his hands as if this was the height of foolishness. "Understand one thing, Devers. There is strength in unity. By the same token, there is weakness in disunity. We would be fools if we permitted ourselves to be weak. You'll have to get out of the valley."

"The hell I will." Rod flung the words at him. "That's what you wanted all along, ain't it?"

Again Abbot faced the others. "You were right, Sam, and I was wrong when I said he'd listen to reason." He walked back to England and Webb, said something to them, and the three of them left the saloon.

For a moment Rod thought that was the end of it, but only for a moment. Now Sam Kane stepped away from the others. Anger had grown in him through these few minutes while Abbot had been talking. His face had turned red and then darkened until it was almost purple.

"Jason's too damned easy," Kane said. "We knew where you stood all the time. You're George Devers' brother and he's Hermann's man. Tonight you had a talk with that Max Sanchez. I guess that adds up."

The others nodded, the tall Larkin saying ominously, "We ain't standing for no traitor living north of Spade."

No, it wasn't over. It hadn't even started. Now Rod realized that this had been carefully planned by Jason Abbot. He wasn't waiting until the first of September. He had worked on these men until they were close to hysteria and now they'd do the job for him if they could. They wouldn't be satisfied with giving him a whipping. They'd run him out of the valley.

Kane said, "You're going to wish you'd pulled out like Jason told you. Now we'll show you what we do to traitors."

Kane started toward Rod, the line of men behind him moving forward. Rod, staring at these men who were his neighbors, knew that Marcia had been right. He didn't have a friend among them. They were a pack of wolves intent on pulling down the man who refused to run with them.

Chapter VI

CLAY CUMMINGS still stood behind Rod and to his left. He had not moved; he had not said anything. There was no doubt about the old man's solid courage, and there could be no doubt about his feelings toward Abbot and Sam Kane and the rest of them. In that moment Rod made his decision. He unbuckled his gun belt and handed it to Cummings.

"Sam's looking for trouble," Rod said, "so I reckon I'll oblige him. Keep the rest of 'em off my back, Clay."

Cummings grabbed the belt, yanked the gun from holster, and laid the belt on the bar. "All right, buckos," he yelled. "If any of you horn into this, I'll let daylight into your guts. Back up, Larkin. You hear me?"

Rod swung around to face Kane who stopped, balancing himself on the balls of his feet. This was not to his liking; he had counted on a dozen men backing his play, but now he was alone, and he had worked himself into a position from which he could not escape without fighting.

Rod said, "You were going to show me something, Sam."

Cursing, Kane lunged at Rod, right fist swinging for his chin. Rod ducked and caught Kane on the nose with his left. It flattened under Rod's fist and blood spurted and the big man cried out in pain. He swung again. Rod stood his ground, taking Kane's blows on elbows and shoulders or rolling his head with each punch. He was the faster of the two, his coordination was better, and he kept pumping his left into Kane's face. They weren't hard blows, but they stung and cut, and in a matter of seconds blood was dripping from Kane's face.

Suddenly Kane changed tactics; he fell forward, hands outstretched; he got Rod by the legs and brought him down in a hard fall. Rod broke free and rolled away; he got to his hands and knees and came on up to his feet. Kane reached out in a futile grab for an ankle. Rod backed away, taunting, "Get up off the floor, Sammy."

Cummings laughed. "You're kind o' old to be playing down there, Sammy boy."

Kane was on his feet then, wiping a sleeve across his blood-smeared face, and lunged at Rod, his fists swinging. Again Rod stood his ground, cracking Kane in the stomach and in the face. For a time they stood there, trading blows, and there was no sound but the thudding of fists on bone and muscle and their panting struggle for breath. Then Kane landed an upswinging right to the side of Rod's face and he went down.

Pinwheeling lights exploded across Rod's vision. Instinct made him roll catlike; he caught the blur of Kane's big boot that missed his head by inches. He rolled again and got up and backed away, the yells of the watching men a crashing roar of sound against his ears.

He had to have time, and he gained it by continuing to back up, doing nothing but block Kane's blows while his head cleared. Kane, overanxious now, kept boring in, swinging uppercuts that never quite landed. Rod, still backing up, ran into a chair and sprawled over it, upsetting a table in his fall. Cards and chips spilled over him. Kane grabbed up the chair and threw it. Rod ducked it, for Kane was a little slow, and one eye, almost closed, was bothering him.

Rod regained his feet, and taking the initiative, drove at Kane. He took a blow on the shoulder; he whipped a short, battering left into Kane's face that swiveled his head on his shoulders, he got Kane again on the cheek bone just in front of his ears, and Kane went down.

"Bust him, Devers," Cummings yelled. "Damn him, give it to him in the guts."

But Rod stood motionless, taking this moment to suck breath back into his tortured lungs. Kane struggled up to his hands and knees; he lifted his head and peered through his one good eye at Rod, then he plunged forward, coming in low, his hands outstretched. Rod drove a knee into the man's face, the sound of the blow a sharp, ringing crack. Kane's head snapped back; he fell away and rolled over on his side and lay there, motionless, his mouth sagging open.

For a moment the room pitched and turned before Rod, and from a great distance he heard Cummings say, "Larkin." Rod lurched to the bar; he laid a hand on it and held himself upright, knowing he had been hurt more than he had realized. Again Cummings shouted, "Damn you, Larkin, are you gonna make me kill you? Stand pat. Devers licked him fair enough."

"He killed him." The tall Larkin had moved out ahead of the

others, bitter and vindictive. "If he did, we'll put a rope on his neck."

"He done what he had to," Cummings snapped. "He sure as hell didn't ask for this fight."

Rod reached for the gun belt and buckled it around him. He wiped sweat and blood from his face. Breath was coming easier now. He said, "You follow Kane's lead and you'll fetch more trouble to this valley than you ever saw."

He backed toward Cummings, seeing that Kane was beginning to stir. He took his gun from Cummings' hand and went on out of the saloon. For a moment he leaned against the wall, the night wind sweet and cool against his battered face. He ran a tongue over his lips, tasting his sweat and blood. His entire body was a great, aching mass of flesh. He opened and closed his hands and rubbed them against his pants' legs, then he went on along the boardwalk to the hotel.

Doll was at the desk when he reeled in, intent only on getting to his room. Doll cried, "What happened to you?" He went on across the lobby to the foot of the stairs, then his knees folded and he fell on the stairs, his feet still on the floor.

"Ma," Doll screamed. "Ma."

Rod didn't lose consciousness, but he had the weird feeling he was standing to one side looking at himself. He heard running steps in the hall, and Marcia asked, "What's wrong?"

"Rod." Doll pointed to him. "He looks like he got wound up in a buzzsaw."

Marcia saw him and she cried out involuntarily. "We've got to get him up to his room."

"Let's get the doc," Doll said.

"Can't. He's out at Larkin's place. Mrs. Larkin is having a baby."

Rod braced his hands against the stairs and pushed himself upright, Marcia and Doll holding to his arms, and oddly enough he thought of Larkin, there in the saloon when he should be home with his wife. Men did funny things. If he had a wife who was having a baby . . .

"You've got to get up the stairs," Marcia said. "Try, Rod."

Doll giggled hysterically. "One step at a time," she said.

Somehow he did get up the stairs, both women holding to his arms and partly lifting him. They turned him along the hall. Doll threw a door open and he went in and fell across the bed.

"Get some hot water and a rag," Marcia said, lighting a lamp. "He's hurt pretty bad."

"I'm all right," Rod muttered. "All right."

Marcia tugged his boots off; he got over on his back and unbuckled his gun belt and arching himself, pulled the belt out from under him and dropped it beside the bed. He lay there for a moment, his mind clearing, and he thought of Cummings.

"Get Clay Cummings out of the saloon," he said. "Fetch him over here."

"He'll be all right," Marcia said. "Let's get your clothes off."

"I ain't so bad off I can't undress myself," he said. "Quit it."

"Deliver me from a stubborn man," Marcia breathed. "You'll probably die saying you're all right."

"Get out of here," he said. "I'll get my clothes off."

She went out and he heard Marcia say something to Doll. He sat up and pulled off his pants; he got out of his shirt and crawled under a quilt, exhausted by the effort. Marcia came in with a pan of hot water and a cloth. She wiped his face and examined the cuts.

"You'll have a scar or two out of this," she said. "You won't be so good looking."

"Too bad." He tried to grin. "I sure was handsome."

"Who did it?"

"Kane."

"I suppose I ought to look at him."

"Yeah, you oughtta see him."

"You hurt anywhere else?"

"No."

But he did hurt, his ribs and his chest and his belly, and each breath brought a sharp pain. Just banged up, he thought, but he wasn't sure. He might have some broken ribs. Kane had hit him a few times in the side.

"I'll have the doctor look at you when he gets back," Marcia said, "and I'd better get word to Spade. You won't be riding out there in the morning."

"I figure I will," he said. "I'll be all right, come morning."

"Stubborn." She stood up, her hands on her hips. "Real stubborn."

He looked at her, managing a wry grin. "I work hard at it," he said. "Funny thing. I didn't know he was hurting me when we was fighting. Seemed like he got in just one real wallop and that one knocked me down."

"More than one." She sat down on the edge of the bed. "Was Jason there?"

"He left before the tussle." He saw that the corners of her

mouth were trembling, and it surprised him, for she had always been a self-possessed woman who held her emotions under rigid control. "Forget it. Nothing to worry about."

"You don't know," she said. "He's poisoned them, Kane and Larkin and all of them. I've heard him in the lobby talking to any of them he could get to listen. He'll use them and he doesn't care how many of them get killed."

"He won't get anywhere," Rod said. "Hermann will straighten them out when he gets here."

"They won't listen, Rod. If you tell a lie often enough, folks believe you, and Jason has told it often. You've been neighbors to these men, but you don't understand them. You're different."

"No different. We all want to own our outfits and a two-bit herd." He reached out and took her hand. "Now quit worrying."

"No, you're different." She let her hand lie in his, her face quite plain now without the sweet curve of the smile that usually touched the corners of her mouth. "You've never been a failure, Rod. These people have. It's their last chance. That's why Jason has been able to work on them. Well, I guess it's natural enough for men like Kane and Larkin to be afraid of anyone like Hermann who is successful."

He had never thought of it quite that way. She was probably right, for it could explain the panic that had turned them into a killer pack. Marcia turned her head and began to cry, and he squeezed her hand, saying, "It ain't your worry. Now quit it." But he knew there was nothing he could say that would do any good. She was suffering an inner agony that he could not touch. She belonged to Jason Abbot, but she hated him, and she would always hate him, and now she didn't know how to free herself.

Marcia rose. "I'm sorry, Rod." She wiped her eyes and turned to face him. "If there is anything a man hates, it's a bawling woman." She swallowed. "I'll kill him, Rod. Before this is done, I'll kill him."

She turned to the door. He said, "Thanks, Marcia."

She stopped and looked at him. "Rod, don't turn against Doll because of me."

He searched for the right words to tell her that he respected her, that he would not hold her relationship with Jason Abbot against her, but it was a hard thing to say, and before he found the words, she was gone.

Clay Cummings came in a few minutes later, his Stetson in his hand, his long white hair brushed back from his forehead.

He walked to the bed and looked down, a grudging admiration in his faded eyes.

"Quite a hassle, Devers," Cummings said. "Kane looks like he ran his face through a meat chopper. Well, I wish I was young and full of vinegar like you are, but I'm old and licked. To hell with it."

"Kane all right?"

Cummings laughed. "He won't be all right for a week. Doll fetched me over here. Said you wanted to see me."

"I wanted her to get you out of there. I was afraid they might take it out on you."

"Naw," he said derisively. "A wolf pack scatters after you knock the leader off, although Kane ain't much of a leader." He pulled at his beard, scowling. "You know, them boys bought a damned poor horse."

"Abbot's a horse trader," Rod said.

"I was thinking the same," Cummings said. "What's that ornery son up to?"

"He's got something up his sleeve," Rod said.

"And it ain't just his arm. Well, I'm going to bed."

"Blow out the lamp," Rod said.

Cummings nodded, and walking to the bureau, blew out the lamp. He left the room, closing the door behind him. Rod lay there, his eyes closed, and presently he heard a band of riders leave town.

Rod's thoughts turned back to what had happened in the saloon before his fight with Sam Kane. The whole thing had been carefully staged by Abbot, with Kane picking the row up as soon as Abbot left. Rod wondered about Kane. Was the man honestly sincere in what he was doing, or was he, like Abbot, striking at Rod for some selfish reason of his own?

Sam Kane was not a likable man, and he wasn't particularly bright. His single track mind would grasp an idea and cling to it with bulldog tenacity. But Rod had never known him to do a dishonest act. He was being fooled, Rod decided, the same as Larkin and the others. As Marcia had said, Abbot had worked on their fears, telling his lies over and over until they were believed,

A feeling of frustration worked into Rod. By fighting Kane, he had saved himself a beating, perhaps a hanging. But he hadn't touched Abbot. The man's position in the valley was stronger than ever, and there was no telling what his next move would be.

Rod was still thinking about Abbot when he dropped off to

sleep. He stirred often, turning from one side of the bed to the other in a vain attempt to find a position where the lumps in the mattress would not aggravate the steady aching of his battered body.

He lay on his side facing the door when something woke him, a slight noise that his sleep-fogged mind could not immediately identify. Then he realized the door was opening slowly. The turning of the knob must have been the noise he had heard.

Stealthily Rod's right hand slid over the edge of the bed. His gun was still in the holster, and he remembered dropping his belt on the floor. The springs squealed just as a man said in a low tone, "Don't move, Devers, and nobody will get hurt."

Abbot! Rod lay motionless, right arm dangling over the side of the bed as Abbot slipped in and closed the door. He cursed himself for his stupidity in not leaving his gun under his pillow, but this was the last thing he had expected. Skillfully playing on the fears of Sam Kane and Otto Larkin and the others so that they would work themselves into a lynch mob was one thing, but for Abbot to come into his room and murder him in cold blood was something else.

Now, with every nerve tense, Rod watched the vague figure of the man who stood not more than six feet from the bed. Rod could not be sure, but he thought Abbot had a gun in his hand. In this one moment, drawn out until it seemed to run on for an eternity, Rod considered rolling off the bed, or making a lunge at Abbot, or groping for his gun which he knew was within inches of his hand.

He had no doubt at all that Abbot intended to kill him, but there was a chance something might happen to give him a better break if he waited. On the other hand, any sort of movement would bring a bullet. Even in the darkness, it was not likely Abbot would miss. So Rod waited, sweat breaking out all over his body, his heart hammering.

"You awake?" Abbot asked.

"I'm awake."

"All right then," Abbot murmured. "Listen to me. I'm here to talk to you."

Rod did not believe him, but if Abbot wanted to talk, it meant he was in no hurry to kill him. Now, fully awake, Rod could make out the man's tall body more clearly, and he was certain of the gun in his hand.

"I'm surprised you're still alive," Abbot said in a low tone that betrayed no emotion. "The way the boys felt, I thought they'd take care of you, but you were lucky Clay Cummings was there to side you."

"And you're sorry as hell," Rod said.

"No," Abbot said. "It's Hermann we're after, Devers, not you. I'm satisfied it worked out the way it did."

He was lying, Rod thought, but there was no point in saying so. Very gently Rod eased closer to the edge of the bed so that his hand touched the floor, but he did not feel the gun belt, and again the springs groaned under the shifting of his weight.

"Don't move, I told you," Abbot said, his voice, higher now, betraying his nervousness. "I'll say what I came to say and you can take it or leave it. You're going to leave the valley, Devers. There's no middle ground about this with you feeling the way you do. I'm willing to buy you out because it's the simplest way of handling the whole business. Get up and dress and come over to my office. We'll take care of everything tonight."

"The price?"

"Anything within reason," Abbot said. "There's one joker. You're to be out of the valley by sunup, and you'll give me your word you will never come back."

There was a falseness about this whole thing that bothered Rod because he couldn't put his finger on it. Abbot was too fond of money to throw even a few dollars away when, by waiting, he might get rid of Rod for nothing.

"I don't savvy," Rod said. "You've got a gun on me. Why don't you shoot me and have it over with?"

"I'd like to," Abbot said. "Don't make any mistake about that. There's just one reason why I don't. It's too dangerous. On the other hand, there's no danger to anyone if you leave the country. How about it?"

"No," Rod said. "To hell with you."

"All right, if that's the way you want it." Abbot's voice was shrill and startlingly loud. "But don't forget one thing. I know your kind, Devers. If you stay, we'll have the damnedest blood letting in this valley the West ever saw and you'll be responsible."

"Are you trying to get rid of me because I threw you out of my place?" Rod asked.

Abbot laughed, a harsh and strident sound. "No. I'm not a little man, Devers, and I don't play for little stakes. You're in my way. That's all."

He left the room, banging the door shut behind him. Rod

made a wide sweep with his hand, found the gun belt, and pulled it up on the bed beside him. He yanked the Colt from the holster and turned over on his back, breathing hard.

He was convinced he had been as close to death just now as he had ever been in his life, but Abbot's reason for playing it as he had puzzled Rod. Perhaps he had lost his nerve. Or maybe England and Webb were waiting outside to cut Rod down the instant he appeared on the street. Or, if he had signed over the Rocking R, they might have followed him out of town and killed him.

The possibility that Abbot was playing it straight didn't add up. Marcia might have persuaded Abbot to make this offer, but whether she'd had a hand in it or not, Rod could not believe it was an honest one.

He got up and propped a chair under the knob and went back to bed. This time when he went to sleep, the Colt was under his pillow.

Chapter VII

W HEN ROD WOKE, it was broad daylight. He got up and washed, being careful not to disturb the scabs that had closed the cuts on his face. He was sore and stiff all over, and he still had a pain in his side when he breathed, but he felt better than he expected.

He dressed and went downstairs to the dining room. Doll was waiting on a couple of drummers when he sat down. Startled, she came to him. "Rod, you've got no business . . ."

"I've got a lot of business." One side of his mouth was bruised and puffy, but the other side was good for a grin. "I get the idea you're worried about me."

"You get a lot of funny ideas," she snapped, and whirled and stalked back to the drummers' table.

"Ham and eggs," Rod called after her.

She took the drummers' orders and walked into the kitchen, ignoring Rod. A few minutes later she brought his plate of ham and eggs and set a cup of coffee beside it. "Doc didn't get back last night. We were going to . . ."

"Don't need him," Rod said. "I'll feel fine as soon as I get this bait of grub inside me."

"Rod, you aren't going to Spade today?"

"You bet I am. Soon as I eat."

"You're tough, aren't you? You're a whole man and team and a dog under the wagon."

She flounced back into the kitchen. Rod ate, wondering if he should talk to Marcia about Abbot's visit, and decided against it. He'd just worry her. She probably didn't know what Abbot was up to. Even if she did, she would not be free to tell him. Or would she? He pondered that for a time. He wasn't sure. But he was sure of one thing. He didn't know all there was to know. Marcia was holding something back.

Doll came in with the drummers' breakfasts and stopped at Rod's table on her way back to the kitchen. When he looked

47

up, he saw that her face was composed. She asked with studied indifference, "What did Abbot want last night?"

Startled, Rod asked, "Why?"

"I couldn't sleep last night. I had my door open and I heard someone in the hall. When I got up, I saw Abbot pussyfooting along the hall toward your room."

"Did he see you?"

She nodded. "I called to him. He jumped about three feet, then he came back to my room and said he just wanted to talk to you and for me to keep quiet. I did, but I stayed up until he left."

"He wanted to buy me out," Rod said, "providing I'd leave the country."

"Funny time to be talking business," she said skeptically. "In the middle of the night."

"That's what I thought," Rod agreed.

She returned to the kitchen. She didn't believe him, he thought. Well, she could think what she wanted to. She probably didn't give a damn about him now, one way or the other. But he owed her his life. He was guessing, but it made sense. Abbot had intended to kill him. He had admitted it was too dangerous. He hadn't explained why, but it was plain enough now. Doll would have known he was the killer.

When Rod finished eating, Doll was not in sight. He went into the lobby, and finding the desk deserted, left two silver dollars beside the register and went out into the blinding sunlight. It was warm even at this early hour, and he thought of the grass in his hay field that would be ready to cut in a few days.

Probably the fence was down and Todd Shannon's cows were in the hay field again. For the first time since the series of "accidents" had started, it didn't make any difference to him. Not unless he could raise two thousand dollars by the first of September. He didn't have much chance of that. He didn't have much chance of staying alive that long, either, the way things were going.

He got his sorrel from the stable, paid the liveryman, and took the road to Spade. He held his horse down to a walk, for the rocking motion sent pain knifing through his side. Half a mile from town he passed a sign that read, "Spade grass. If you don't have business on it, you're trespassing."

Clay Cummings had put that sign up years ago. George had left it, although there was no real reason for it. Up until now, the small ranchers had been satisfied to get along without antagonizing the one big layout in the valley.

The grass looked good. By late summer it would be belly high on a horse. It had been an empty country when Clay Cummings had come north from California with his herd and Mexican vaqueros, and he had chosen well. The country here was floor-like, and in the late spring Egan Creek, fed by rain and melting snow in the Blue Mountains, flooded the center of the valley. It was the best kind of natural irrigation, and Cummings had never lacked grass.

The road angled southeast, following a low ridge that bordered Egan Lake. Rod had made this ride once shortly after he had come to the valley when Cummings, making his last desperate try to recoup his lost fortune, was holding on and hoping for a good beef price in the fall. But it hadn't come, and now, thinking about the old man who had tamed this country, it seemed to Rod that there was no fairness about it.

Karl Hermann had taken advantage of Cummings' bad luck just as he had taken advantage of Bill Devers' bad luck years before. The difference was that Rod's father had never been anything but a small rancher, so when Hermann's bank had taken his spread, it had gained nothing but a quarter section of patented land and a waterhole along with some graze that Bill Devers had used because no one else wanted it. But when Hermann bought Clay Cummings out, he'd bought an empire. There were at least ten thousand head carrying the Spade iron, and with proper management, Hermann could double the number.

The lake stretched out before Rod, acres of tule marsh bordering it that was muskrats' heaven. Birds, too. Ducks, geese, swans, cranes, even the precious egrets that had brought fortunes for more than one transient hunter who had come here for them. Now, riding along the north edge of the marsh, another thought occurred to Rod. The tule marsh, drained and cleared, would make the best hay land in the world.

Hermann was a careful man, insisting that his ranches carry hay from one year to the next so they would never be caught without a winter's supply. If Cummings had operated that way, he might not have been beaten, for his heavy winter losses had combined with low prices and his bad selection of race horses to whip him.

Rod reached the west edge of the lake and started across the dike that Cummings had built when he had first come to the valley. A sand reef lay to his left, holding back the waters of Egan Lake. If the reef ever went out, at least five thousand acres of what had been lake bottom would be exposed to the sun and might eventually be the home of fifty or more families. But the question of ownership was a knotty one and had been a subject of debate in the Palace and Marcia's hotel lobby for hours at a time.

Rod crossed the bridge that spanned Halfmile Creek, the slow-moving water making a liquid whisper of sound in the morning silence. Alkali Lake with its white-crusted shore lay below the bridge, gray and forbidding, the final receptacle for the mineral carried by the valley streams. It held no life, a strange, barren pool in a valley of plenty.

A band of mallards flew over Rod, hitting the water of Egan Lake and skidding to a stop. A blue heron stood in the shallow water along the edge, motionless, stilt-legged. An avocet flew by, making the air melancholy with its cry.

Rod, riding up the sharp slope south of the lake, wondered if George liked it here, a strange country to a man raised on the dry Nevada rangeland. Rod shook his head, thinking he wouldn't swap his quarter section on the mountain slope with its pines and spring and view of the valley for all of Spade.

He rode into the ranch yard, noticing little change from the time he had been here before when Cummings had owned it. The sprawling white house shaded by tall poplars that Cummings had planted in the late sixties, the huge barns and sheds built when nails were not available, their sides held together by rawhide, and the maze of stockade corrals that were peculiar to this country. They were made by setting juniper posts close together and threading willows between them, the strongest and longest-lasting corrals that could be made according to Clay Cummings.

Thinking of the labor and hopes and dreams that had gone into the building of this ranch, Rod could not understand how Cummings had been able to take his loss as casually as he had. If the old man held any bitterness toward Karl Hermann, he hid it behind a mask of affability, saying he'd taken a licking and someone else would have gobbled him up if Hermann hadn't.

Spade appeared to be deserted, although that seemed unlikely in view of the fact that George had sent for Rod. Then he heard someone banging at an anvil in the blacksmith shop, and almost in the same instant an old Mexican came out of one of the barns. He moved toward Rod who had dismounted and was watering his sorrel, his swarthy face creased by a toothy grin.

"*Saludos, amigo,*" the Mexican said. "*Senor* Devers, he is expecting you. Go in. I will care for your horse."

"Thanks, Juan," Rod said, and turning, walked along the row of poplars to the front door of the house.

The old Mexican was Juan Herrara, one of the few vaqueros still alive who had helped Clay Cummings drive his first herd to Egan Valley. When Cummings had made the sale to Hermann, he had stipulated that Juan was to be given a home on Spade as long as he lived. Actually he was receiving what amounted to a pension for past services. Now in failing health, nothing was required of him except a few easy chores around the barns and corrals.

It was a small act of kindness on Hermann's part, a promise he could easily have forgotten once the transaction with Cummings had been completed. But he hadn't, and Juan was happy while he waited to die, content with a bunk and three square meals a day and the assurance he would be taken care of. Rod had never thought of it before, but now it struck him that Hermann had something in his makeup besides his love for wealth that seemed to dominate him so completely.

The door opened before Rod reached the porch and George stepped out, calling, "Glad you're here, boy. Didn't hear you ride up." He stopped, startled. "If I didn't know you were a good rider, I'd say your horse piled you into a juniper. What happened?"

"I tangled with Sam Kane last night."

George crossed the porch and held out his hand. "Well, I'm awfully glad you got here, Rod. I was a little afraid you'd say to hell with it."

"I might have if Marcia hadn't been curious about why Sanchez wanted to see me."

George frowned as if trying to place someone named Marcia. He was shorter than Rod and too pudgy for a man still in his early thirties. His eyes were gray like Rod's, and his hair was very nearly the same medium brown except that he was getting a little bald in front which added to his appearance of middle age. There the resemblance ended. He had none of Rod's quick grace, none of his long-boned lankiness, and he possessed none of the violent temperament that characterized Rod.

He said, "Marcia" in a slow, thoughtful way, and then nodded as if finally identifying her. "Mrs. Nance, the hotel woman?"

"That's right. Sanchez was waiting for me in the bar and she sent me to see him."

"She's supposed to be Abbot's woman, isn't she?"

"So the gossips say," Rod said shortly, irritated by the question.

"I know," George said. "I guess it's the same everywhere. People make a lot of nothing. I know what they've done about Mr. Hermann, and none of them know a damned thing about him." He swung toward the door. "Come in, Rod. No use standing out here in the sun."

Rod followed him into the living room, the irritation in him growing. George, he thought, was giving him a mild reprimand about his attitude to Hermann. It rubbed him the wrong way, too, George always referring to his boss as "Mr. Hermann."

Rod dropped into a leather chair just inside the door, knowing that the nagging pain in his side and the soreness which the ride had aggravated made him more edgy than usual. But he hadn't come here to quarrel with George. He put his hands on the arms and sat back, his gaze swinging around the room.

Everything about Spade was unusual, even this living room. The mantel above the cavernous fireplace held a dozen brands belonging to the big outfits that lay south along the Steens and out into the desert toward the Wagon Wheel country. The furniture was heavy and black, thick drapes added to the gloom, and even the expensive Brussels carpet was dark blue. The room depressed Rod, and he wondered how George was able to live here.

"Like the room?" George asked.

"No."

"Didn't think you would." George sat down on a black leather couch. "I've left it the way it was, but if Grace doesn't like it, we'll change it."

"You mean this is the way Clay left it?"

"That's what I mean. He thought he was doing everything up brown when he got this furniture and carpet. Cost a fortune." George drew a cigar from his coat pocket. "Fixed it up for his wife. You don't know the story?"

"No, never heard it."

"Clay thought his wife would come up here and live, but when the time came, she couldn't stand it, living in a wilderness with her nearest neighbor ten miles away." George shrugged. "Well, I guess nothing made much difference to Clay after that."

Rod nodded, thinking that it explained Clay Cummings' attitude. In one way he was like Juan Herrara, waiting to die. He had done a tremendous thing, bringing the first herd to the valley, but now in the twilight of his life, it meant nothing to him.

A sudden impatience was in Rod. He asked, "What did you want me for?"

George took the cold cigar out of his mouth and stared at it, turning it slowly between his fingers. He said, "I've got no blood kin but you, Rod. I've been here for two years, and the only times I've seen you were when we met in town by accident. I'd like to change that."

It was the most surprising thing he had ever heard his brother say. George was not given to a show of emotion, and Rod had always supposed that their relationship was the way George wanted it. Even when George had come to the valley to visit him, they had found little to talk about. Later he had learned that George's real purpose in coming had been to make Cummings an offer for Spade, knowledge which had not made Rod think any better of him.

There was a tight moment of silence, then Rod said, "I guess we ain't after the same thing."

"No, that was always the trouble." George looked up, the tip of his tongue touching dry lips. "You've always been a one-track man. You learned to handle a gun because you could make good money as a gunslinger and you wanted money to buy a ranch. As long as I can remember, the only thing you wanted was your own outfit."

"And you never did."

George spread his hands. "No. I was satisfied to get on Karl Hermann's pay roll. It's worked out pretty well for me. I've got one of the best jobs in his company."

Rod watched George get up and walk to the door, his face troubled. It was the first time he had ever seen behind the mask of cool certainty which George habitually wore, the first sign of doubt his brother had ever let him see.

"Looks to me like you don't have a worry in the world," Rod said. "I've got enough for both of us."

George leaned a shoulder against the door jamb, the cigar tucked between back teeth, his brooding eyes on Egan Lake. He said, "I've got more worries than you'd ever guess. Rod, has it occurred to you that you might be wrong about something?"

Surprised, Rod said, "Hell, yes."

"I mean about Mr. Hermann. You blamed him for taking

Dad's spread, but afterwards I found out he didn't even know about it. He owns five banks, and as long as they're making a profit, he doesn't bother them."

A thought that had been nagging the back of Rod's mind took definite form. He had been like Sam Kane and the others, jumping to the conclusion that because a man had started with nothing and become a millionaire, he must be a thief. Kane's attitude had been ridiculous, wanting to fight before he knew whether he had any reason to fight.

Now, here in the cool, depressing gloom of Spade's living room, Rod mentally admitted he had been as obstinate and stupid as Sam Kane and the others. He hadn't tried to find out anything, either. He only knew that Karl Hermann had owned the bank which had taken his father's place, therefore he had assumed that Hermann was responsible.

"Maybe it was that way," Rod said.

George wheeled to face him. "I never thought I'd hear you say that."

"I reckon Kane addled my brain." Rod grinned with the good side of his mouth. "Or maybe it's a proposition of comparing Hermann to somebody else. Jason Abbot, for instance."

George walked back to the couch and sat down. "Alongside Abbot, Mr. Hermann is a cousin to the Lord Himself." He swallowed. "Rod, I've worked for the Hermann Land and Cattle Company for nine years. In that time I have never known it to order a murder or rob a man or deal unfairly with its neighbors."

"That's a little hard to swallow."

"I've got to make you believe it because I sent for you to offer you a job. Mr. Hermann needs you, although he doesn't know it."

"The hell!" Rod leaned forward in the leather chair. "You know I'll be putting up hay in a week, but you fetch me here to offer me a job."

"So I'm a knuckleheaded idiot. Well, I had to try, Rod. I'd kind of like for you and me to be on the same side."

Rod sank back against the leather. "Go ahead. Maybe I'll let that hay go."

A slow grin broke across George's face. "I didn't think I'd hear that from you." He took the cigar out of his pocket. "Mr. Hermann and Grace will be here tomorrow. They leave Gouge Eye early in the morning and I want you to meet them on the pass which should be about noon. I'm hiring your gun, Rod. It's a job I wouldn't offer to any other man."

"You could meet him yourself," Rod said. "Why hell, you've got a dozen men you could round up."

"I don't want to start the ball, Rod. That's just what I'd do if I showed my face in Poplar City."

"Take your crew . . ."

"I said I didn't want to start it. Anyhow, my boys are scattered from here to the Steens and out in the desert. I haven't got time, and Mr. Hermann would raise hell if I did. He thinks a buckaroo's job is to look after cattle."

"What makes you think I can do the job?"

"I don't think, Rod. I know. I've followed everything you did from the day Dad died, and I've been both proud and envious because I'd like to be the kind of man you are, but I never had it in me."

Rod rolled a smoke, his eyes on the brown paper that he twisted and sealed. He fished a match from his pocket and lighted the cigarette, taking his time. He could not believe he'd heard the words George had just said, George who had always been so sure and smug and a little self-righteous.

"Speaking of things you never thought you'd hear," Rod said finally, "that's something I never thought I'd hear."

George gave him a wry grin. "I wouldn't say it if I didn't need your help. The valley men are your friends. With you riding beside Mr. Hermann and Grace, they won't have any trouble."

"I ain't your man," Rod said. "I don't have a friend in the valley."

"I can't believe that . . ."

"I told you I had a fight with Sam Kane."

"You're still my man," George said stubbornly. "You'll get Mr. Hermann to Spade without trouble. I want you to stay here till he leaves, and I don't have any idea when that'll be."

Rod rose. "I've got a spread to run. Ain't much, but it's all I've got."

"Name your figure."

"Might take all summer."

George nodded. "It might."

"Two thousand dollars. I'll stay here till he leaves the valley."

Rod had been sure that would end it, but without the slightest hesitation, George said, "I'll get it for you."

George left the room, returning presently with a bulging money belt that he handed to Rod. "This is the easiest way for you to carry it. Better count it."

"I'll take your word for it."

"Why did you want two thousand dollars?"

"That's what it takes to get Abbot off my neck."

George accepted that, not asking for an explanation. He glanced at his watch. "I'll go tell Wang to put another plate on the table." He started toward the dining room, then turned back. "Rod, I think you'll wind up liking Mr. Hermann."

"You mean you're hoping."

"Maybe. I like him and I respect him, or I wouldn't have stayed with him for nine years. He's got more guts than any other man I know. One time I saw him go up to a man who held a gun on him and take the gun away from the fellow. For anybody else it would have been stupid, but not for Mr. Hermann."

George left the living room then. Rod moved to the door and stood looking at the blue, placid water of Egan Lake, but he wasn't actually seeing it, for he was thinking of the expression he would see on Jason Abbot's face when he gave the horse trader the money.

Chapter VIII

THE SUN was barely showing above the eastern hills when Rod had breakfast in the hotel dining room the next morning. Neither Marcia nor Doll were up. Ada Larkin brought Rod's order to him and returned at once to the kitchen. She was a tall, bony woman who found it hard to smile. Now, for some reason, Rod thought how seldom he had heard laughter except from Doll and Marcia during the three years he had lived in the valley.

When he was done eating, he left half a dollar on the table and went out into the cool, windy morning. Later the day would be hot, but at this hour the night chill still clung to the air. It was one of the things Rod liked about the country, and was at least partly responsible for the absence of disease among the cattle.

Rod saddled his sorrel, thinking he had ample time to reach the pass before noon. He rode down the street and reined up in front of Abbot's office, not sure the man was up. He'd get Abbot out of bed if he was still sleeping, for he wanted to free his mind of the worry that owing money to Abbot had aroused in him.

He stepped down and racked his horse, hearing a rooster crow from a chicken pen on a side street. Someone was chopping wood, the sound of ax on pine carrying sharply to him through the thin air. As he stepped up on the walk, the swamper came out of the Palace and slung a bucket of dirty water into the street. Nodding a greeting, he asked, "How do you feel this morning?"

"I'm still a little sore," Rod answered.

The swamper laughed. "I reckon Kane is, too," he said, and went back into the saloon.

Rod tried the door of Abbot's office. It was locked. He knocked, and when there was no answer, he hammered on the door, wondering if Abbot had spent the night on his ranch. Then the lock clicked, the door swung open, and Abbot stood staring at Rod. His hair was disheveled and he was wearing only his pants and underclothes. Rod found it hard to believe that this peevish man was the same tall, dignified Jason Abbot who had skillfully maneuvered the small ranchers against him that night in the Palace.

"Find my note," Rod said. "I'm paying you off."

"Go to hell," Abbot said waspishly, and started to shut the door.

Rod shoved a boot across the threshold. He asked, "What's the matter with you? I've got the money."

"Pay up when the note's due," Abbot said, still trying to shut the door.

Rod put a shoulder to the door; he drove against it and slammed it open, knocking Abbot halfway across the room. Rod went inside, unable to make any sense out of this. He said, "You sure wanted your dinero the night you were out to my place. What changed your mind?"

Abbot scraped the tip of his fingers across his pointed chin, making a sandpapery sound in the silence, dour eyes pinned on Rod's face, then he whirled and lunged toward his desk. He yanked a drawer open and was bringing a gun up when Rod reached him. He hit Abbot on the chin, slamming him back from the desk and turning him half around. Abbot fell against the wall, his feet sliding out from under him, and he sat down hard, the gun dropping from his hand.

Rod picked up the gun and stepped back. "You out of your head, Abbot?"

"Yeah, maybe I am." Abbot got up, pulled his swivel chair back from the desk, and sat down. "Devers, this country's too small for both of us and I'm not leaving. That means you are."

"I don't figure that way." Rod placed Abbot's gun on the desk. "Get your gun belt, Abbot, and come outside. We'll fix it so we won't be crowding each other."

"I'm not that big a fool," Abbot said thickly. "There are other ways of going at this."

"Like sneaking into my hotel room to plug me while I was asleep?"

"That wasn't why I went into your room," Abbot snarled.

Rod shrugged. "Have it your way. Get that note out and mark it paid. I've got the money."

"Where'd you get it?"

"My business."

"The only place you could get it is Spade." The wild hatred

that had gripped Abbot's face was replaced by an expression of triumph. "So you've gone over to Hermann like we said."

"I'm going to meet him and his girl this morning, which ain't no never mind to you. Do you want your dinero, or not?"

"I figure the interest at forty dollars. Got that, too?"

"You said you . . ."

"You didn't take my offer." The sense of triumph grew in Abbot as he watched Rod's face. "Go back to Spade for another forty dollars."

A sinking feeling of defeat crept into Rod's belly. His pride would not permit him to ask George for more money. He said bitterly, "You've mudded up my spring and knocked my fence down and burned a haystack. It won't work. I'm staying, but I'm damned curious about why you want the Rocking R."

"I don't. I want you out of the country."

"Why?"

Abbot motioned to the door. "Get out. I'm busy."

Rod didn't move for a moment: he stood staring down at Abbot, hating him as he had never hated any other man. He thought of Marcia and pitied her. He said, "You're the one who had better get out of the country. If you don't, I'll kill you."

He wheeled out of Abbot's office and mounting, left town at a gallop. When he had gone a mile or so, he glanced back and saw that a rider was leaving Poplar City, heading north toward Sam Kane's SK. Abbot, or some rider he had hired to go after Kane. Well, it didn't make any difference. Whatever Abbot planned to do might just as well be done today.

The country began tilting upward, the rocky eastern rim of the valley covered by rabbit brush and a few stunted junipers. It was poor graze that no one claimed, although the day might come when it would be used, and then Rod remembered Sam Kane saying that Egan Valley was about the last place where a man could bring a few head of cows and get a start. Now only hardscrabble range was left, a fact that probably explained why Sam Kane and the others felt the way they did.

Near noon Rod reached the summit and reined up. He sat his saddle, studying the narrow, crooked road that looped back and forth on the eastern slope below him and was finally lost in a maze of canyons ten miles away. Rod had a bad moment, thinking that George had been mistaken about the day of Hermann's arrival, or that something had happened to him and his daughter.

Presently a buckboard appeared around a bend below him,

and Rod grinned a little, wondering why he had become anxious about the welfare of a man he had hated for nine years. But that was the strangest part of the whole business. This thing had become so twisted that he was beginning to look upon Karl Hermann as an ally rather than an enemy.

Dismounting, Rod tied his sorrel to the lone juniper that grew on the wind-swept summit. He sat down on a rock beside the road and rolled a smoke, considering the tree, shaggy-barked and twisted as only a juniper can be twisted. Half of its limbs were dead, but still it clung to life in this dry, sterile soil. A man would make out, Rod thought, if he had half the guts that this juniper had.

Rod was still there when Hermann's buckboard wheeled up the last sharp pitch to the summit and stopped, Hermann eyeing Rod speculatively. Rod rose and walked to the rig, his hand extended. He said, "I'm Rod Devers, George's brother. George sent me here to fetch you to town."

"George's brother," Hermann said with honest warmth. "I've heard of you, Devers. Heard a lot of you. Glad to know you."

Hermann gave Rod's hand a quick grip and then wrapped the lines around the whipstock. He stepped out of the buckboard, stretching, sharp eyes on Rod as he motioned to the girl in the seat. "My daughter Grace, Devers. Probably George mentioned she'd be with me."

Rod nodded and touched the brim of his Stetson. The girl was wearing a linen duster and a floppy-brimmed hat that was tied to her head by a scarf. The wind tugged at it, and she raised a hand as if afraid the scarf wouldn't hold. Rod could tell little about her looks because a combination of hat brim, scarf, and up-turned duster collar almost masked her face.

"How do you do, Mr. Devers," the girl said. "I hate wind. Does it always blow in this country?"

"Not so much in the valley." He turned to Hermann who was standing beside the front wheel, his eyes on the valley below him. "You'll have trouble in Poplar City. Do you want to swing around the town?"

Hermann stood motionless as if he hadn't heard. He was the strangest looking cowman Rod had ever seen. He was in his middle fifties, short of body and pot-bellied, and his round, rosy face seemed a little comical under his black derby hat. He was wearing a brown broadcloth suit and button shoes, and if Rod had not known who he was, he would have mistaken the man for a drummer. There was nothing about him, not even the team of bays or the ancient buckboard, that resembled one hundred million dollars.

"Quite a sight," Hermann breathed in awe. "I'd heard about Egan Valley, a long time before I bought Spade, but it's taken me all this time to get here. Mighty pretty, ain't it, Grace?"

"Yes, Daddy, but did you hear Mr. Devers' question?"

"Question?" Hermann swung to face Rod. "I'm sorry. What did you ask me?"

"You'll have trouble in Poplar City. Do you want to swing around the town?"

Hermann smiled, his blue eyes twinkling. "We will not only go through the town, but we will eat dinner there. We had breakfast before sunup."

"Do you have a gun?"

"I never carry a gun." Hermann was suddenly grave. "Trouble's your business, ain't it?"

"No," Rod answered. "Not any more. I'm a cowman, Hermann. I own one critter to your ten thousand, but we're both cowmen. Trouble ain't my business no more than it's yours."

The girl laughed. "Well said, Mr. Devers. For years I've been looking for a man who wasn't scared of Daddy. At last I've found one."

Hermann's eyes were twinkling again. "She's always looking for men, Devers, of one kind or another. She collects them, you know." He scratched his fat nose. "You're on Spade's pay roll?"

"That's right."

"Then why ain't you taking care of my cattle instead of riding up here to meet us?"

"I was hired to meet you and ride to Spade with you. I suppose you would say that trouble is my business as long as you're in this country, but I took the job for just one reason. I needed money."

Hermann shook his head. "I don't understand George. He knows how I feel about things like this." He shoved his hands into his pockets and rocked back and forth on his feet. "As I remember it, you did not agree with George about going to work for me. Seems like you got your neck bowed about my bank taking over your dad's place. Happened nine years ago, I believe."

"You've got a good memory." Rod shrugged. "I still don't agree with George. He wanted a job with a big outfit. I wanted my own outfit. When you boil it all down, I reckon that's the real difference between me and George."

Hermann nodded. "I suppose it is. Well, I ain't one to say whether you or George is wrong. He's been loyal to me." He glanced at the gun on Rod's hip. "But I have an order against my men carrying firearms. Take yours off and throw it into the buckboard."

"Your orders don't apply to me," Rod said. "Maybe you'll savvy what I mean when we get to Poplar City."

Rod turned on his heel and walked to his horse. He mounted and rode back. Hermann was in the seat again, the lines in his hands. He said stiffly, "I won't have a man working for me who won't take my orders. You're fired."

"Daddy," the girl cried. "You don't know . . ."

"I have certain principles," Hermann said. "I never deviate from them."

"Your principles make money," Rod said, "which same don't mean you know anything about the folks in Egan Valley."

"You're being stubborn, Daddy," the girl said hotly. "Talk to George before you fire this man."

"All right, I'll talk to George," Hermann agreed reluctantly, "but if you expect to stay on Spade's pay roll, you'll do what I tell you."

Hermann spoke to his team and drove down the grade, Rod riding behind the rig. George had said Karl Hermann had more guts than any other man he had ever known, but Rod could not believe that. The girl had called it right. Hermann was just stubborn. If he expected to impress Kane and Larkin and the others, he was mistaken.

They reached the valley floor, and Rod, touching up his sorrel, rode around the rig and took the lead. He had no idea what Kane and his bunch would do, but they'd be in town, waiting, probably a little drunk and certainly filled with Abbot's poison. Rod, from his own experience, knew there was no combination that was more certain to bring trouble than whiskey and hatred which stemmed from fear.

Chapter IX

DOLL WOKE EARLY the morning the Hermanns came to the valley, but she did not get up at once. She thought of Rod, sleeping at the other end of the hall, so close and yet so far away. She could not bear to think of the years ahead without Rod; she had a strong feeling that their quarrel had been a silly one and she was largely responsible for it.

Even now she could not entirely blame herself. She had been afraid of Abbot as long as she had known him, and she hated him because of his affair with her mother. It was an evil thing because he was evil.

She hated Abbot all the more because her fear of him was largely responsible for her break with Rod. She felt unclean every time he looked at her. As long as she lived here with her mother, she could not get away from Abbot. So she had forced herself upon Rod without telling him why it was so important to her to be married now. How could she tell the man she loved about her own mother? Oh, he knew part of it, all right, but only a part.

But she wasn't willing to let it go this way. If she could talk to him, perhaps she would know what to say. At least she could tell him that marrying him next fall was better than not marrying him at all, and she hadn't really meant what she'd said the night she'd gone out to the Rocking R.

She got up and putting on a maroon robe, tied it loosely around her. She'd get Rod out of bed and talk to him. She had to fix it up now because he might leave early to go back to the Rocking R and she'd miss him. She opened the door and ran down the hall to his room, her bare feet making no sound on the thin carpet.

Doll tapped on his door. When there was no answer, she turned the knob and shoved the door open. He was gone. The bed had been slept in, but it was empty now. She leaned against the jamb, sick with disappointment. Only a moment before she had been filled with the wild hope that all she had to do was talk to him and everything would be all right again.

She crossed the room to the window and looked down into the street. When she saw Rod's sorrel in front of Abbot's office, she felt a sudden breaking of the tension that had gripped her. He was still in town! He'd probably come back to the hotel for breakfast.

She started to turn from the window and then swung back. "he saw Rod leave Abbot's office, walking fast, his back too straight, and she knew from the way he untied his sorrel and stepped into the saddle that he was violently angry. He headed east at a fast pace.

Doll returned to her room and dressed quickly, a nagging uncertainty in her mind. She could think of no reason why he would go to Abbot's office, or why he would ride east when there was so much to be done on the Rocking R. Then, hopefully, she wondered if he had left a message for her. She ran back along the hall and searched his room, but there was nothing.

She walked aimlessly to the window, knowing she hadn't really expected to find a message. He probably hadn't given her a thought. She had no right to expect him to, not after all that had happened between them.

The bed in the adjoining room squeaked as a man turned in his sleep. Chuck England, probably. Abbot kept the room rented for his men to use when they stayed in town, and she remembered that England had come in late the night before. She hadn't seen Barney Webb. He might be at the ranch, or he might have slept in Abbot's office.

She was still staring into the street when Webb rode out of the livery stable and turned north at the end of the block. He was riding fast, too, as fast as Rod had been when he'd left town. She walked out of the room, trying to guess what was happening, but there seemed to be no pattern to it.

Ada Larkin was waiting on a drummer when Doll came into the dining room. Doll asked, "Did Rod get breakfast?" Ada tipped her head in a half-inch nod and stomped into the kitchen, cross because Doll should have come down to help her an hour ago.

Ada had never been in love, Doll thought as she walked along the hall to her mother's room. She never would be. She'd marry some man and have a lot of children just as her mother was doing, a man who didn't amount to anything, someone like her father who would rather tomcat around town than stay home when his wife was having a baby.

She tapped on her mother's door, something she had been taught to do when she was a child. She had not understood why then, but she did now, and it added to the smoldering rage that was in her. Jason Abbot might be here.

She had never fully understood why her mother was this way, although she sensed vaguely that it went back to the time when her mother had known Karl Hermann. Something had happened that made her mother hate Hermann with an unforgiving passion that was totally unlike her, for Marcia Nance was a woman who loved far easier than she hated.

"Come in," Marcia called.

Doll opened the door and saw that her mother, still wearing her nightgown, was seated in front of a mirror brushing her hair. Doll said, "Good morning." Marcia turned her head to give Doll a smile, but it wasn't a good smile, just a forced curving of the lips.

Quickly Doll crossed the room and put an arm around Marcia's shoulders. Her mother deserved to be happy, but she wasn't, and Doll knew she was partly to blame, she and Rod.

"What's bothering you, honey?" Marcia asked.

"Rod's gone," Doll said. "I saw him leave Abbot's office. He rode out of town, going east. Why would he go that way?"

Marcia rose and slipping out of her nightgown, began to dress. "I don't know," she said.

"A little while after that Barney Webb left town." Doll stared at the floor where a sharp ray of sunshine coming through the east window fell on a worn, rag rug. "He rode north. It means something, doesn't it?"

"Maybe, but I don't know what," Marcia answered.

She knows, Doll thought, but she doesn't want to tell me. She heard someone coming down the hall, and turning her head toward the open door, she saw Jason Abbot standing there, tall and straight, green eyes pinned on her, his thin, sharp-featured face resembling a coyote's more than ever. He was a coyote, Doll thought, with a coyote's mind, sly and scheming and sneaking along as if he were working his way toward a henhouse on his belly.

"Good morning, Doll," Abbot said. "You are strikingly beautiful this morning."

"Knock the next time you come in here," she said sharply.

He smiled. "I never knock on this door." He turned his gaze to Marcia. "I heard some interesting news this morning."

Marcia breathed, "Well?"

"This is your day," Abbot said. "Devers stopped at my office to tell me he was going to meet Karl Hermann."

Marcia was very pale. She seemed to be paralyzed, unable to move or say what she wanted to say. Doll cried, "Get out of here, Abbot. Can't you leave us alone?"

"No, we're into this together," he said. "Your mother is a very intelligent woman, Doll. When you want to cut grass, you sharpen your sickle. Your mother has used her hone on me until I have a razor's edge. I'll cut the grass today." He laughed, a low sound that was faintly mocking. "I sent Barney to bring Kane and the other boys to town."

Marcia took a step toward him and stopped, her hands fluttering nervously at her sides. "What are your plans, Jason?"

"It will be more interesting for you if you don't know." The smile that had been clinging to the corners of his mouth was gone now. He paused, eyes briefly touching Doll's face, then swinging back to Marcia's. "I don't savvy, but it seems that after all you've done to get ready for this day, you suddenly have an attack of conscience."

"Yes, I have," Marcia said, "But it's for Rod, not Hermann."

"I know," Abbot said. "That's why I'm not telling you my plans. You can't seem to understand we've got to remove Devers if we're going to get at Hermann."

For a moment Doll, shocked by the implication of Abbot's words, could do nothing but stand there and stare at him, then she leaped at him, screaming, "If you touch Rod, I'll kill you."

Abbot caught her wrists and held them. He shook her, a burst of fury touching his cheeks with its torch. "Someday you'll see what Devers is," he shouted, "and you'll see what I am and you'll thank me for what I've done."

"Let her go," Marcia cried.

"She's not going to scratch me up like a bitchy wildcat. I've got plans, Marcia. Your plans." He licked his lips and reluctantly released his grip on Doll's wrists. "Now you listen to me, Doll, and you'll know why you're going to thank me. Hermann has a daughter with him."

"What's that got to do . . .," Doll began.

"Everything." He paused, letting her see the malice that crowded him. "Why do you think Devers has put off marrying you? Well, I'll tell you. He's known for weeks that Hermann was coming with his daughter. She divorced her husband, so she'll be looking for a man. She's what he wants, not you. You can't bring a fortune to him."

He stepped back, watching Doll warily, but she stood motionless, staring at him, not wanting to believe him but still unable to call him a liar. She didn't know what Rod had said to Abbot. Then, thinking back over these weeks, she was shocked by the knowledge that Rod had begun to give her excuses about the time the rumor had hit the valley that Hermann was coming.

"You see how it fits," Abbot said softly. "He isn't good enough for you, Doll. Not many men are."

Wheeling, Abbot stalked along the hall. Doll stood motionless, listening as he climbed the stairs. Marcia came to Doll and put an arm around her. She said, "He's lying, honey. You know Rod too well to believe that."

Doll wanted to cry; she wanted to tear something with her hands, to scream what she'd do to Rod if it were true. Then the moment of near hysteria passed and she moved away from her mother. "I'll go upstairs and change the beds."

"Doll, listen to me," Marcia cried. "Jason's lying. Don't let it upset you."

"Is the Hermann girl good looking?"

"I don't know, and it doesn't make any difference. If you believe Jason's lies, you'll never get things patched up with Rod."

Doll went upstairs, realizing that for the first time in her life she was jealous. She didn't have any right to be, now that she had broken off with Rod, but she was whether she had any right or not. It was not a thing she could be logical about.

Abbot had said, "You see how it fits." That was the trouble. It did fit. Rod's brother had worked for Hermann for years. Probably Rod had seen the Hermann woman. If she was good looking . . . But perhaps that didn't make any difference. She had a fortune, all right. If Rod married her, he'd own an outfit. Fifty of them. He'd be the biggest cowman on the Pacific Coast.

She went into the room Rod had occupied and stripped the bed. She heard the rumble of talk from the next room, Abbot's voice and then England's. Abbot said, "I'll be here when they hit town. There's a chance Devers will run, but we can't count on it. If he doesn't, it will look better if I'm out of town when you throw down on him."

"You know damned well he won't run." England's voice was

sharp. "We'll have to plug him, and when we do, you'll be a hell of a lot safer if you ain't in town."

"I'm not afraid, if that's what you're getting at," Abbot shouted, angry now. "You've got no reason to squall. I've paid you and Barney . . ."

He stopped as if remembering someone might be in the next room. Doll sat down on the bed, her eyes closed. She was jealous and hurt and angry. Still, she couldn't let them murder Rod. But what could she do?

Chapter X

WHEN ROD reached the edge of town, he saw the line of horses racked in front of the saloon. He swung his sorrel back and reined in beside the Hermann's buckboard. He said, "Your trouble's waiting for you. Let me do the talking."

Irritated, Hermann said, "I never have trouble. One of my principles is to get along with my neighbors."

"Maybe it's your principle, but it ain't theirs."

Abbot and Kane came out of the Palace, Larkin and the other north valley ranchers following. They moved into the street to form a solid line of sullen, dark-faced men, all but Abbot armed with rifles or shotguns. Rod ignored them, and reining in before the hotel, stepped down and tied his horse. Hermann had pulled up to the hitch rail, and leaning forward, wrapped the lines around the whipstock.

"I judge you boys are my neighbors," Hermann said pleasantly. "I want to get acquainted with you before I leave town."

Rod walked to the buckboard, his eyes on Abbot. Rod could not read the man's hard set face, but it was his guess that Abbot would build this up as far as he could safely and then step out just as he had the night Rod had fought Sam Kane.

"Take your daughter inside," Rod said in a low tone. "Order your dinners. I'll be in afterwhile."

"I want to talk to these men," Hermann said truculently.

Rod did not look at Hermann. He saw that Barney Webb had come out of the Palace, but England was not in sight. Kane leaned forward and spit into the dust, his face still raw and bruised from the beating Rod had given him. Abbot said something to Kane and Kane motioned to Larkin. Webb remained where he was, but the others fanned out to form a semicircle in the street.

"That's close enough." Rod's right hand dropped to gun butt. "I'll kill the first man who comes any closer."

They stopped, their faces filled with uncertainty. Even Abbot, as neatly dressed as ever and carrying himself with his usual dignity, seemed at a loss as to the next move. For a moment there was no sound but the thin whine of the wind as it played against the eaves of the buildings facing Main Street, then Grace Hermann broke the tension with, "We'll go inside, Mr. Devers. Come on, Daddy."

Still Rod did not move until Grace and her father had stepped down from the buckboard. Then Hermann, standing on the boardwalk, said, "If these men have a grievance against Spade, I want to know what it is."

Kane stiffened, his rifle swinging toward Hermann, and Abbot's right hand darted into a coat pocket. Rod called, "Stand pat, all of you."

A single hot word, a threatening motion would set this thing off. If it broke, Rod knew he would die, but Jason Abbot would die, too, sobering knowledge that held him motionless. Rod heard the Hermanns across the walk; he heard the lobby door slammed shut by the wind.

"You've put on quite a show, Jason," Rod said. "Now if it's talk you want, you and Sam and Larkin come into the lobby."

"No use to talk. I think Hermann got the idea." Abbot pointed a long forefinger at Rod. "I have done everything in my power to get you out of the valley, Devers. Once you're gone, Hermann can be handled."

It had gone exactly as Abbot had planned. He didn't want trouble yet, maybe not any time today; then it occurred to Rod that Hermann might be able to accomplish something if he could talk to these men, at least drive a wedge between Abbot and the others.

"Abbot's talking hogwash," Rod said, "and you boys are smart enough to know it. Come inside and tell Hermann . . ."

"I said there was no use to talk," Abbot snapped. "Hermann got a good look at us. He knows that if he starts pushing, he's in for trouble."

Wheeling, Abbot stalked back toward the Palace. Kane touched a bruise on his cheek, baleful eyes on Rod, then he turned and went into the saloon, the rest following like the sheep they were, Rod thought bitterly. Only Barney Webb remained, his cold, confident eyes fixed on Rod's face.

"The boss ain't had much luck getting you out from under foot," Webb said. "Now I'm taking the job over. I'm giving you an hour to get to hell out of town. Keep going till you're out of the valley."

Webb turned on his heel and went into the Palace. Rod tied Hermann's team, wondering how fast Barney Webb was with a gun. Well, he'd soon know. He walked into the hotel and sitting down at the Hermann table, gave Ada Larkin his order.

When Ada disappeared into the kitchen, Rod nodded at Grace. "Thanks for getting your dad out of the buckboard. You've got more sense than he has."

She had taken off her linen duster and hat. She was wearing a black suit, and now that Rod had a close look at her without the scarf which had hidden part of her face, he saw she was a fine looking woman, a little older than he had thought, and fully matured. Her rich, red-lipped mouth curved easily into a smile; her blue eyes twinkled as she looked at Rod.

"Daddy hates to admit that, Mr. Devers," she said, "but I agree with you. I am smarter than he is."

Hermann scowled. "Stop your bragging. I'm smart enough." He looked at Rod. "What's wrong here, Devers?"

"They're afraid of you," Rod answered. "It's that simple. They think you're going to grab the whole valley, and the way they see it, the easiest way to protect themselves is to put you out of the way."

"I don't need the damned valley," Hermann said hoarsely. "I'm going to tell them . . ."

"You think they'd listen?" Rod demanded. "Or if they did, do you think they'd believe you?" He shook his head. "Look, Hermann. Little men are afraid of big men. You must have been up against it before."

"I've always been able to talk to men," Hermann said. "Go fetch the leaders over here. I can make them believe me."

"Won't do you no good to get me killed," Rod said. "My job is to get you to Spade alive. Maybe you don't care about your own hide, but you've got your daughter to think about."

Grace smiled at her father. "That's right."

"But I don't savvy," Hermann said. "They don't have any grounds for their suspicion. I want to tell them the truth."

"What you tell 'em won't prove anything," Rod said impatiently. "If you can figure out a way to show 'em you want to be a good neighbor, you can prove your intentions, but they won't believe anything you say if you talk for a week."

"The people in this valley don't know me," Hermann said bitterly. "I want them to, Devers, and I want to know them."

Rod leaned back in his chair, impatience at Hermann's stubbornness growing in him. He could not tell the cattleman what Marcia had said about Abbot, and Hermann did not realize that his reputation had grown until he had become a sort of terrifying legend to the valley settlers.

"Do one thing," Rod said after a moment's silence. "Don't jump the traces until I get you to Spade. Talk to George."

"But you know . . ." Hermann began.

"Daddy," Grace interrupted, "you do what Mr. Devers says. It's George's job to tell you, not his."

Glowering, Hermann shifted his weight in his chair and reached for a cigar. Ada Larkin came out of the kitchen, her heels tapping sharply on the floor. Rod thought she was bringing their dinner, but when he looked up, he saw that her hands were empty.

Bending over him so that her mouth was close to his ear, she whispered, "Mrs. Nance wants to see in you in her parlor."

She whirled and walked rapidly back to the kitchen. Rod hesitated, glancing at Hermann, then he rose. "Excuse me," he said, and left the dining room.

He walked down the hall to Marcia's parlor, feeling a little uneasy. At this time of day Marcia was usually behind the desk, and Doll always waited on tables through the dinner hour. He wondered if there was some reason for them not wanting Hermann to see them. The door to Marcia's parlor was open, and he went in.

Marcia was sitting in her rocking chair and Doll was standing by the window. Both were pale and plainly nervous. The uneasiness grew in Rod, for it was not like either of them to be nervous, and he could not see any reason for it. What had happened in the street was no concern of theirs.

"Sit down," Marcia said.

"I haven't got time," Rod said. "I left the Hermanns waiting at a table."

"I know," Marcia said. "It won't hurt them to wait."

"Not unless the Hermann woman finds it hard to do without your company," Doll breathed. "I guess I know why you don't want to marry me."

He stared at her, not understanding. She was glaring at him, her temper edgy, and he could see no hint of the bouncy, gay humor which ordinarily dominated her. Because his own nerves were taut, he said more sharply than he intended to, "You should. I've told you enough times."

"Maybe you haven't told me the truth," Doll snapped. "Maybe you're looking for bigger game."

He understood then. Hot words were on his lips. He checked them, sensing that both Doll and Marcia were under some strain which he didn't know about.

"Did you fetch me back here to talk about that, Marcia?" Rod asked.

She shook her head. "Doll's imagination is working over-time." She lowered her eyes to her hands that were clasped on her lap. "Rod, I wouldn't say this if I wasn't convinced you were in love with Doll. I don't want you killed for that reason, but you can't blame Doll for thinking what she does. If you do love her, you'll save your life, for her."

He leaned against the door jamb, looking at Marcia and then at Doll. "I don't know what a man needs to do to prove he's in love with a woman." He brought his gaze back to Marcia. "I took the job George gave me because it's the one way I can get Jason Abbot off my neck. I've got to finish the job. I've already been paid."

"You don't have to finish the job," Marcia cried. "The main thing you've got to do is to keep on living. If you go back into the street, you'll be killed. Let the Hermanns go on by them-selves, Rod."

He was certain now that there was something here he didn't know, something they wouldn't tell him. The thought struck him that Marica had a stake in Abbot's game, that part of the things she had said the other night when he'd had his fight with Kane had been lies, or at best, only part of the truth. He said stubbornly, "I made a deal with George. I'll keep my part of the bargain."

He wheeled and walked back down the hall. He heard Doll cry out, "Rod, Rod . . ." But he kept on, and crossing the lobby, went into the dining room and sat down. Ada had brought the Hermanns their dinner. Now she came out of the kitchen with his steak and coffee, and walked away, her face still barren of expression.

They ate in silence, Hermann sour and Grace appearing to enjoy the excitement of the moment. Ada brought their pie a few minutes later, and when they were done, Hermann rose. "Let's get moving, Devers."

"No hurry," Rod said, glancing out of the window. The street was empty, but if Barney Webb was waiting for him, he'd show the instant Rod appeared in the street.

Hermann stopped by the lobby door and took his derby hat off the rack. He said, "I'm in a hurry."

"You're following orders," Grace said sharply. "Remem-ber?"

Hermann put his derby on his head, saying nothing. Ada came out of the kitchen and he paid her for their meals. Grace slipped into her duster and tied her hat on her head with her scarf. Then she asked, "You think there will be more trouble?"

"Yes. Stay inside the lobby till I tell you to come out." Rod drew his gun from holster and replaced it; he glanced at Hermann's stormy face. "We have no law here, which is something you'll have to get used to. We're too far from the county seat for the sheriff to bother with us."

"I'll change that," Hermann said harshly. "I'm paying enough taxes to deserve some protection."

"You're getting protection," Rod said, and went out into the sunshine.

The street was still empty, then he saw Barney Webb come out of the Palace. He called, "Devers."

Rod moved along the boardwalk until he reached the end of the hitch pole. For three years he had been a rancher, slow years without violence. It was the life he wanted. All the time when he had been earning gunfighter's wages, his mind had reached ahead to the day when he could hang his gun up. Now he was back to where he had been, and the strangest part of it was that he was fighting for Karl Hermann.

The old poison of hatred was gone. Hermann was not a man who was easy to hate. Rod had been wrong and George had been right except for one thing. He idolized Hermann to the point where he exaggerated the man's power and courage. Up here Hermann's wealth and power could not save him. Only Rod's gun could do that.

Rod did not say anything to Webb. Words would be wasted. Webb had stepped down off the walk, his pale blue eyes on Rod. He stood waiting, tense, expectant. The wind still cried around the eaves of the buildings; it picked up a haze of dust and carried it down the street. Somewhere in a back lot a rooster crowed. A bucket was lifted off a bench by the wind and banged against a wall. A dog barked. A child called out and another answered.

They were ordinary sounds that seemed to come across a great distance to Rod's ears, common peaceful sounds that had nothing to do with gunfire and death. In this strange, drawn-out moment they seemed to symbolize the three years Rod had spent on the Rocking R. Now it was as if these years had never been. Time had made the complete turn.

In the sharp afternoon sunlight Rod saw Barney Webb's face clearly, a thin, tight-featured face that needed a shave, the calculating blue eyes that were like the eyes of so many gunmen Rod had known. Suddenly fear touched Rod as he wondered if the three years had slowed his draw, then the fear was gone. He could not afford it. He had to kill. He had too much to live for to let Webb kill him.

Rod took a slow step forward, right hand hovering over gun butt. Webb had never seen Rod pull a gun. Uncertain of his superiority, he had let this play out, hoping that Rod would break, that in a crazy burst of panic he would go for his gun and throw a wild shot. But Rod had never given way to panic and he didn't now. He took one more step and it was Webb who broke under the pressure, his right hand sweeping down toward his gun.

The two shots hammered out, drowning all the little sounds; powderflame danced from gun muzzles and died. It was close, terribly close, Webb's bullet slicing through Rod's vest under his left arm pit. A few inches to the right and Rod would have been a dead man, and it would have gone there if Rod had not had a slight edge in speed.

Webb was partly turned by Rod's bullet; his knees gave under him and he fell, his hat coming off his bald head as he went down. He rolled over on his left side, lips tightly drawn against his teeth. He had dropped his gun. Now he gripped it again and tilted it, and once more Rod fired and Webb's face dropped down into the dust.

Rod did not move. He held his smoking gun, eyes on the batwings of the saloon. He wondered where Chuck England was, where Jason Abbot was; he was not sure what Kane and his friends would do. Then the batwings were flung open, and Kane came out, Larkin and the others behind him.

"You boys taking this up?" Rod called.

Kane stood over Webb's body, hating Rod and fearing him, but sobered by what had happened. He said, "Not today. Get out of the country, Devers."

"Where's England and Abbot?"

Kane did not answer. He knelt beside Webb's body and felt of his wrist, and then he rose. He was not man enough for the job he had given himself, and he plainly showed that he felt the overpowering weight of his own futility. He shouted in a high, crazy voice, "Get out of town, Devers. Take the Hermanns with you."

Rod knew this was no time to talk, no time to try to pound any sense into Kane's stubborn mind. Without turning his head, he called, "Hermann." This was as much of a safe conduct as he would ever get. Later Kane would regret what he had done, but at the moment, standing beside Webb's body, he was incapable of taking a stand.

Hermann and Grace came out of the hotel; they got into the buckboard and drove down the street. Quickly Rod untied his sorrel and stepped into saddle, his gun still in his hand. The stunning impact of death held Kane and his bunch motionless, but it might not last. Rod dug steel into the flanks of his sorrel; he caught up with the Hermanns at the edge of town before he holstered his gun.

"What kind of a damned wild country is this?" Hermann shouted.

"You should have looked into it when you bought Spade," Rod said. "Ask George."

Grace looked at him, her face still flushed with excitement. "You're a brave man, Mr. Devers."

"Not brave," he said impatiently. "A man does what he has to do and in my book that ain't bravery."

They were silent then, Rod riding beside the buckboard. He was a little weak now that it was over, and sick with the knowledge that this was only the beginning. One death led to another, once the first blood had been shed, for that was the pattern a thing like this invariably followed, and no man, Rod or Jason Abbot or anyone, could tell where it would stop.

Chapter XI

For a time Rod was so lost in his thoughts that he ignored the Hermanns. A question kept nagging his mind until he was driven frantic by the elusive answer. Where had Chuck England been during the fight with Barney Webb?

Rod did not waste any time wondering about Jason Abbot. The horse trader had probably been in his office, or he might have gone to his ranch. But regardless of where he had been personally, he certainly had done everything he could to make sure Rod was killed. Why, then, had Barney Webb been given the job while England remained out of sight?

Now that he had time to think about it, Rod had the feeling Webb had been very sure of himself when he had stepped out of the Palace. Several seconds, perhaps a minute had passed before he pulled his gun.

Recalling the expression on Barney Webb's face and the way he had played for time, it seemed to Rod that the gunman had become less sure of himself as those seconds passed. Was it possible that England was supposed to come into the play and something had held him out?

Rod shook his head, exasperated. He could not think of anything that would have kept England out of the fight. It was hard to believe that he would have remained inside the saloon after Webb was down and Kane and his bunch had come into the street; it was equally hard to believe that anything could have gone wrong with Abbot's plan, whatever it was.

They had swung west along the north shore of the lake, and now they reached the sand reef and Hermann pulled up. Rod, jerked out of the deep well of his thoughts, was only then aware that they had almost reached Spade and that Hermann was leaning forward in his seat, eyes on the lake.

Grace gave Rod a tolerant smile. "He's hypnotized himself, Mr. Devers. We are about to see a new thought being born."

Rod reined up in the grass beside the buckboard. He nodded and was silent, not having the slightest idea what was in Hermann's mind. But something was churning there, and it occurred to Rod that Hermann was both a dreamer and a practical man, a rare combination that perhaps accounted, at least in part, for the fabulous success he had made.

Some sandhill cranes were engaged in a crazy, flapping dance. Slender avocets gave out their melancholy cry. Curlews, long-billed and nosey, talked in their "curlee" language. A belligerent Canada goose honked a challenge and was immediately set upon by a trumpeter swan and soundly beaten. Then the swan came up on the shore, arching his wings and strutting as if he had accomplished a great thing.

Grace laughed and glanced at Rod again. "A three-ring circus," she said, and Rod nodded.

Hermann apparently had not seen the show. He said, "Looks like a lot of shallow water along the shore. If that sand reef went out, there would be a sizable piece of lake bottom exposed. It would be a chore to drain it and get rid of the tules, but it could be done."

Rod nodded again, still silent. An observing man, this Karl Hermann. In these few minutes he had hit upon the same idea that everyone in the valley had talked about, but apparently the question of ownership had not occurred to him. Rod did not feel called upon to mention it. The sand reef had been here a long time and it would probably continue to be here, but if Hermann took it on himself to blast a channel in the reef, he'd find himself with more trouble on his hands than he had now.

Hermann swung a hand in a wide circle away from the lake. "Looks like it's all George said it was, Devers, but I'm wondering about something. Is the valley land ever flooded?"

"It is along the streams," Rod answered. "That's why you always have the grass."

"And hay," Hermann said thoughtfully, "but if we had this marginal land drained, we could raise hay here and we'd have more grazing land. Isn't that right?"

"Sure," Rod said, "but I suppose you've got a million acres of mountain and desert graze. The bunch grass that's native to this country is the best there is. You don't need any more."

"Not for the size herd I have now," Hermann agreed, "but I didn't make my money by being satisfied with what I have. Well, I'll see what George says."

Hermann spoke to the team and the buckboard wheeled on across the dike, Rod reining in behind the rig. A few minutes later they crossed the bridge that spanned Halfmile Creek and went up the sharp slope to Spade's yard.

George came out of the big ranchhouse, calling a greeting. Grace waved to him, but Hermann sat motionless, staring sourly at George.

"Welcome to Spade," George said genially as he came to the buckboard.

"It's beautiful," Grace said. "The best ranch we own. You didn't exaggerate it a bit."

George held up a hand and helped Grace down; he put his arms around her and kissed her. Rod, surprised at this greeting, thought there was little ardor in the way Grace returned the kiss. She stepped back from him and motioned toward her father.

"You're looking at an ungrateful man, George," Grace said.

Hermann wrapped the lines around the whipstock and stepping down, offered his hand. "I've seen some things today I don't like, George."

If George was bothered by Hermann's attitude, he gave no sign as he shook his employer's hand. "I know, Mr. Hermann, I know exactly what you're thinking, but you're safe and sound. I'll admit I was worried."

"You had cause to be," Rod said drily.

"George, you know . . . ," Hermann began.

"Stop it, Daddy," Grace interrupted angrily. "If it hadn't been for Rod, we wouldn't be here."

George pinned his eyes on Rod. "Trouble?"

"Plenty. Abbot and Kane were waiting in town with their bunch. Hard to tell how far they intended to go, but after we had our dinner, Barney Webb jumped me. I killed him. If he'd got me, your boss would have been in for it." He nodded at Hermann. "He's an ungrateful cuss for a fact."

Hermann drew his shoulders back, his face red. "Damn it, George, it's not that I'm ungrateful. I don't know what the trouble is, but you've let it get out of hand. That's what I don't like."

"Come in and I'll tell you what's been happening," George said, still maintaining his composure. "Juan, take care of the horses. Mr. Hermann, this is Juan Herrara. He was with Clay Cummings when Clay drove his first herd into the valley."

Juan had come out of the barn. He bowed and grinned toothily. "*Saludos, mi patrón,*" he said.

The frostiness thawed from Hermann at once. He walked toward Herrara and held out his hand. "I remember Clay speaking about you, Juan. I'm glad to know you."

Pleased, the old man bobbed his head.

Rod, watching, felt an increased respect for Karl Hermann. Out of the thousands of men who worked for him, he remembered his agreement with Clay Cummings about Juan Herrara. Another reason for his success, Rod thought. A man in Hermann's position had to have loyalty, and this touch of kindliness was probably typical of him and accounted for the loyalty which a smaller man would never have.

Hermann turned with Grace and George toward the house. Rod said, "I'll take care of my horse."

"Come in as soon as you can," George said. "Supper is almost ready."

Rod took his time, not knowing what would be expected of him now, and preferring to stay in the bunkhouse. He smoked a cigarette, loitering for a few minutes in the shade of a poplar, the sun well over toward the west. He thought of Doll and Marcia, wondering how Marcia had known what Barney Webb would do. She must have, or she wouldn't have said he'd be killed if he went back into the street. There could be only one answer. Abbot had told her his plan. That reminded him of the other question that had been bothering him. What about Chuck England?

Resentment touched him when he thought of Doll, and her insinuation that he had put off their marriage in the hope of making a better one with Grace. He was used to her violent and willful moods, but he had never known her to be jealous. Well, she had made herself plain enough. He could not hope that their relationship would ever be the way it had. Perhaps it was his fault, tying together as he had his ambition to own a ranch and his love for Doll.

She had said she wouldn't come second to a ranch; she had to be first or nothing. She hadn't understood, she hadn't even tried. If he could have lived these last few days over, he would have made the same choice. She was selfish, he thought bitterly. She wanted her own way just for the sake of having it. So he had lost her and perhaps it was just as well. Or better.

He flipped his cigarette stub away and went on to the house. No one was in the living room, but he heard George and Hermann talking in the office. Rod went back to the porch and sat down, his back against a post.

He heard heels click on the porch, and turning his head, saw that Grace was coming toward him. She had put on a black velvet dress, a little too low cut, he thought, and a little too tight around the hips, an expensive dress that did exactly what she wanted it to do for her. It was quite plain except for a lace ruffle around her throat and the row of white buttons down the front. She wore a pearl necklace that probably represented a small fortune.

As he rose she asked, "Like it?"

"Sure. Looks about like ten thousand dollars."

She smiled. "Not quite. I'm wearing it for you."

"I thought it would be for George."

A small smile touched the corners of her mouth. "We'll let him think so, but . . ."

She stopped, her head cocked. Inside the office Hermann was shouting, "Damn it, George, what's got into you? Two thousand dollars for a few hours of a man's time. You keep saying that bunch of settlers would have killed me. That's loco. I wanted to talk to them, but your brother never gave me a chance."

Grace's face turned bitter. "Come inside, Rod. George needs help."

She whirled and went back into the house. Reluctantly Rod followed, thinking that this side of Karl Hermann was exactly what he had expected. Grace crossed to the door of the office which opened into the living room.

"You'd better fire me," George said. "I did the only thing I could because your safety is more important than any amount of money. You simply don't understand the feeling that's in the valley."

"Then it's your fault for letting it . . . ," Hermann stopped, aware that Grace stood in the doorway.

"You're being stubborn again, Daddy," she said softly. "And downright foolish. I was with you, too, you know. It might have been different if you were alone."

"But George paid his brother two thousand dollars just . . ."

"Just to save our lives," she broke in. "Rod Devers has already earned it if he doesn't do another thing."

Hermann ran a hand through his hair, glaring at Grace, and then suddenly the anger flowed out of him. "You're right. Forget it, George."

"Am I fired?" George asked.

"Hell no. You're the last man in my organization I'd fire."

George wheeled and walked out. He said to Rod, "You'll want to wash up."

Rod said nothing while he followed George down the hall to the back porch. After he had washed, he found a comb and ran it through his hair. George, watching him, said, "You've seen several sides of Mr. Hermann today."

"Reckon I have. Well, you can have your life. I'm satisfied with mine."

"But he's not what you thought he was, is he? You don't hate him, do you?"

For some reason Rod's answer seemed important to George. Rod said, "No, I guess you were right about Dad losing his place. I mean, I don't think Hermann knew anything about it."

"I'm sure of it," George said.

They went back down the hall and into the dining room where Hermann and Grace were already waiting. It was a quiet meal, a little too grand for Rod with the shiny silverware and the candlelight and the lace tablecloth, but it suited George, and Rod found himself wondering what George's relationship with Grace was. She had gone out of her way to tell Rod she was wearing the velvet dress for him and not George, but she didn't want to tell George. Well, it was their business, Rod thought. As soon as he finished up his part of the bargain, he'd be glad to get away from Spade.

When they returned to the living room, twilight was moving across the valley. George lighted the pink, hobnailed lamp on the mahogany table in the middle of the big room and turned to Grace.

"I haven't changed anything in the house since Clay moved out," he said. "How do you like this room?"

She was sitting on the leather couch, slumped wearily, her legs stretched in front of her. She said, "It's an amazing room to find out here in the middle of nowhere, George, but the whole house and the ranch are amazing. I'd like to meet Clay Cummings."

"You will," George said. "Clay's in town, and he'll stop on his way back. He always spends a night here. I guess he likes to look things over. Still home to him, I suppose."

Hermann lighted a cigar, and walking to the fireplace, threw the match into it. He stood there, looking at George, and it struck Rod how much alike they were. In another twenty years George would resemble his employer even more than he did now.

"I want to see this country, George," Hermann said. "Really see it because I'm convinced that what we have here is just a beginning. While we're riding around, your brother can look after Grace."

Grace smiled. "I was hoping it would work that way."

Rod's agreement with George did not include running herd on a girl, but before he could say so, a man called, "Devers." It was a familiar voice, but for a moment Rod could not place it.

George wheeled toward the door, his face pale. "Excuse me," he said, and ran out of the room.

"Who's that?" Hermann asked. "More trouble?"

"I don't know," Rod said, and moved to the door.

A man was standing beside the poplars in front of the house, the reins of his horse in his hand. Rod's breath was jolted out of him as if he'd been struck in the stomach. It was Todd Shannon, the shifty-eyed, furtive Todd Shannon who belonged to Jason Abbot. Then Rod remembered what Sam Kane had said about George being behind the "accidents" that had been plaguing him. It couldn't be true, Rod thought, but what other reason would bring Shannon here?

Chapter XII

Rod slept in the bunkhouse that night, or tried to sleep, but the hours dragged out while he lay staring at the black ceiling, his body rigid. Irritated by Juan Herrara's gurgling snores, he got up and sat for a time in the doorway and smoked a cigarette, hardly aware of the night sounds; the hooting of an owl, the mournful cry of a bird from the lake, the yapping of the coyotes on some distant rim.

George had given no explanation when he had returned from talking to Todd Shannon. If he realized that Rod had recognized Shannon, he gave no indication of it. Rod could not be sure, but it seemed to him George looked both guilty and worried when he came back into the house.

Rod considered himself a reasonably tough man. Now he told himself he'd been soft to believe George when he'd said, "I've got no blood kin but you. I've been here for two years, and the only times I've seen you were when we met in town by accident. I'd like to change that."

Well, it might be true. He wanted Rod here where he could watch him. Or use him in some way which was not yet apparent. If the visitor had been anyone but Todd Shannon . . .! Rod thought about Marcia saying Jason Abbot wanted to murder Karl Hermann. Could Shannon be a connecting link between George and Abbot?

Rod returned to his bunk, telling himself it was impossible, that George was not the kind of man who would be involved with Abbot, that his loyalty to Hermann was beyond question. But no amount of self-assurance could blot out the suspicion that was in Rod's mind. There simply wasn't any explanation of Shannon's visit except the one which Rod refused to accept.

Rod ate breakfast in the cookshack with Herrara and the blacksmith and Pablo Sanchez who had ridden in late the evening before. Herrara harnessed Hermann's team and hooked up, and George left with Sanchez and Hermann, still offering no explanation. Grace would want to take a ride later in the morning, George had said, and he'd ordered Herrara to throw a side saddle on a bay mare named Lady.

Grace did not make her appearance until after ten. She came out of the house wearing a tan riding skirt and a broad-brimmed hat; she moved with quick, easy grace, her blue eyes bright with good humor. She was attractive and desirable, and very much a woman. Rod found himself liking her, even against his will.

The first day set the pattern for the following days except that Sanchez returned to the cow camp. Hermann and George took the buckboard, or a two-wheeled cart when Hermann wanted to see the desert west of the valley; they were always gone until sundown, taking a lunch with them, and when they sat in the living room after supper, Hermann's good humor seemed to grow daily.

One evening in the middle of the week when Rod was alone with George, he asked, "How long are the Hermanns staying?"

"They haven't said," George answered.

"You hired me to look out for Hermann," Rod said irritably. "Instead of that, I turn out to be Grace's riding partner."

"You'll have your chance to look out for Mr. Hermann," George said somberly. "He's bound to see Abbot and Kane and the rest of them. Thinks he can straighten everything out by talking to them." He paused, eyes pinned on Rod's face, then asked, "Can he?"

"Not as long as Abbot's alive, and Kane and his neighbors trust him."

"That's what I thought." George scratched an ear, smiling a little. "You're not objecting to being Grace's riding partner, are you?"

"No, but hell, anybody could ride with her."

"You're wrong on that. She's a hard woman to satisfy." George scratched his ear again, his face going sour. "She's falling in love with you, Rod. You're lucky. Or maybe unlucky, depending on how you look at it."

George wheeled and walked away. Rod watched him, thinking this was the damnedest thing he'd ever heard. He was no lady's man, and Grace was about as likely to fall in love with him as a cow was to grow wings.

After that he was often aware of her eyes being on him, studying him, and she had a sort of proprietary attitude toward him. She insisted that he eat dinner with her in the house instead of the cookshack, and even when they came in from their rides, he found it difficult to get away from her. She lingered around the corrals or the barns just to be with him, and Herrara always seemed to disappear.

Once she came into the bunkhouse when, for lack of anything better to do, he was sitting at a table playing cards. She said frankly, "I know a woman isn't supposed to be out here, but I don't see any sense in sitting in the house by myself."

She lay down on a bunk, her head propped up on one hand, her skirt pulled up to her knees. Rod went on playing, trying to pretend he was unaware of her shapely legs and the high mounds of her breasts that pressed tightly against her blouse.

She wasn't like Doll, he thought, who, when the mood was upon her, would josh him about how cold the winter nights were when a man slept alone. Grace was more subtle. Without saying a word, she let him know that all he had to do was to reach for her.

That's exactly what he would do, he told himself, if it wasn't for Doll, and immediately admitted that was no reason to ignore Grace. Doll was done with him. Still, he found himself wishing Grace would go back into the house where she belonged.

She laughed softly. "Put those cards down, Rod. After all, you don't have a woman visitor in the bunkhouse very often."

"No." He laid a red queen on a black king, not looking at Grace. "You make it rough on a man."

She laughed again. "You've got that wrong, mister. You make it rough on a woman." She was silent, her face suddenly grave, then she said, "George tells me you have a little ranch in the foothills."

He nodded. "The Rocking R."

"I'd like to see it."

He glanced up, startled. "I can't take you off Spade range, not with things the way they are."

"Things won't be this way much longer," she said. "Daddy doesn't like trouble. He'll get it fixed up some way, even if it costs him a lot of money."

Money wouldn't touch Jason Abbot, Rod thought as he went on playing. George should tell Hermann. But he probably wouldn't, not as long as he was being blamed for the trouble.

"You're not like George at all," Grace said. "He's very practical and a little dull. You're interesting, Rod. I suppose it's because you're kind of mysterious. You don't talk much."

He laid his cards down. "Nothing to talk about." .

"Yes, there is. George says you want your own place. Isn't that kind of foolish when you could have a good job with us?"

"It's all in the way you look at it," he said sharply. "According to George, it is."

She sat up and swung her feet to the floor. "You might change, Rod. Daddy needs a man like you." She rose and rubbed her back side, smiling wryly. "I hope my saddle isn't as sore as I am, but I'm getting tough. Tomorrow Wang is fixing us a lunch. I want to ride into the mountains."

She went out. Rod didn't finish his game. There was no fun in it now. He rolled a smoke, tipping his chair back. So she thought he would change when he was this close to accomplishing what he wanted. Well, she was crazy if she thought that.

Suddenly he felt an urge to saddle his sorrel and ride out. He wanted to see the Rocking R again. Maybe the grass was right for cutting. If he stopped in town, he'd see Doll. Then the desire died in him. He didn't really want to see her. He left the bunkhouse and drifted aimlessly toward the corrals, restless and impatient with this monotony.

That night after supper there was a sudden and unexpected break in the monotony. They were in the living room, Hermann telling Grace about the desert where he and George had been that day, when a rifle cracked from the other side of the poplars, the bullet smashing through a window and burying itself in the opposite wall, missing Rod by inches.

Rod made it to the table in three long strides as two other rifles opened up; he blew the lamp out and plunged on to where Grace was sitting in one of the big, leather chairs. He pulled her to the floor, roughly, having no time to explain anything. The three rifles were throwing lead as fast as triggers could be pulled, and some of it was coming through the open door and windows.

"Get down, Hermann," Rod called. "You, too, George. On your bellies."

For a moment he lay on the thick Brussels carpet, Grace in his arms. She murmured, "Well, this is one way to get you to notice me."

"I've been noticing you," he said. "Now crawl into the dining room. Stay down."

"I can use a gun . . ."

"Do what I tell you." The firing stopped and Rod heard Hermann swearing bitterly. "Got any guns handy, George?"

"In the office," George answered. "I'll get them."

Rod got up and lunged toward the nearest window, drawing his gun as he ran. Abbot was out there, he thought, probably with England and Todd Shannon. If that was all, the attack was just a gesture designed to stir Hermann into some sort of action against the north valley ranchers, but if they were all out here, it meant Abbot had convinced them that the best defense was attack. With only the blacksmith and Herrara in the bunkhouse, it might be a long, hard night.

George handed Hermann a Winchester and moved to one of the windows. He asked, "How do you figure this, Rod?"

"Can't tell yet," Rod answered, a little surprised that George was taking this as coolly as he was.

"I want a gun," Grace called. "You hear me, George."

She had followed Rod, making no sound on the carpet, and now she stood at his side. He shoved her away from the window into a corner of the room, demanding, "What the hell are you doing here? I told you to . . ."

"And I said I can use a gun," she flung at him. "Let go of me."

"Get down . . ."

Then Abbot and his men cut loose again. Rod wheeled back to the window, swearing softly. She stood a good chance of getting tagged, for the house had not been built for defense and some of the bullets were getting through.

Three riflemen out there. No more. Rod breathed easier as he emptied his Colt at the flashes. This was not an attack in force, or there would be fifteen men instead of three, and by this time they'd be rushing the house if they meant business. Hermann and George were firing from the other windows, then there was a lull, and Hermann called, "More shells, George."

Tough enough in a pinch, Rod thought, and grinned as he reloaded. Outside a man yelled, "Hermann, can you hear me?"

It was Abbot's voice. When Hermann didn't answer, Rod called, "We hear you."

"It's Hermann we want," Abbot shouted. "Listen, you thieving bastard. This is the 99. We won't stand for you taking our spreads. We'll wipe you out the first move you make. Savvy?"

"Do it now," Hermann shouted. "Come and get us if you've got the guts to try."

"This is just a warning," Abbot called.

Hermann opened up with his Winchester, but Rod and George held their fire because they could not see anything to shoot at. Hermann was just giving vent to his feelings, Rod thought. When his rifle was empty, the sound of hoof beats came clearly to Rod. He said, "They've gone. Light a lamp, George."

"It's a trick," Hermann snarled. "Let's go after them."

"No use," Rod said. "This wasn't the small ranchers. It was just one ornery son named Jason Abbot and a couple of boys who take his pay."

A match flared in George's hand. He lighted the lamp and replaced the chimney, looking across the room at Rod. "What was he after?"

Grace still stood in the corner where Rod had pushed her. She was angry and she made no secret of it. "I'm mad enough to kick somebody. I told you I wanted a gun."

Rod didn't look at her. He said, "It was Abbot's way of making Hermann think the little fry is gonna push, but I've got a hunch he couldn't talk 'em into coming with him. Chances are they're waiting for Hermann to push."

Hermann slammed the butt of his rifle against the floor. "By God, I will if that's what they want."

"It's not what they want," Rod said. "It's what Abbot wants."

Hermann sat down, glowering. "A hell of a note. I've got no reason to grab anything that isn't mine, but I'm not going to stand for them riding in and shooting up my property. Look at those windows."

"I'll have Herrara fix them in the morning," George said.

Now, looking at Hermann's set face, it occurred to Rod that Abbot might have accomplished more than he realized. To be attacked for no reason at all was the one thing that would make Hermann hard to deal with.

"You're up against one man," Rod said, "not the whole bunch you saw in town."

"One man, you say," Hermann said bitterly. "Then you'd better go after him if you're going to earn that two thousand dollars."

"I aim to," Rod said, "but I'll pick my time." He turned to Grace. "Still want to take that ride tomorrow?"

"Of course," she snapped.

"Then I'm going to bed," Rod said.

"I'll stay up," George said. "Might be a trick."

Rod and Grace left early the next morning, riding south across the grass, the lunch sack tied behind Rod's saddle. George was still asleep. Hermann, still furious over the unprovoked attack, said he'd stay at Spade.

They reached a gap in the hills before noon and followed Bearclaw River for a mile, then stopped and ate the lunch Wang had fixed for them. Clouds had been building up along the eastern horizon. Rod watched them uneasily, thinking a storm was overdue.

"We'd better go back," he said, "or we'll get wet."

"You're not sugar or salt," Grace jeered. "You won't melt." She stared down into a deep pool at the dark, shadowy trout. "There's one down there a foot and a half long, Rod. We should have brought our fishing poles."

"You don't know what our summer storms are like," he said doggedly. "We ought to head back."

"I'm not afraid of storms." She looked at him, her face upturned, her red lips slightly parted. "Rod, I want to meet Cummings."

"You will. What made you think of him?"

"Something George said the other evening. About Cummings building the house and furnishing it for his wife who couldn't stand it to be alone, so she left him. I feel sorry for him. I mean, when a man does that much for a woman, she must be pretty cheap and small to just go off and leave him. I wouldn't, not if I loved him."

He turned away and walked toward the horses. Without knowing it, Grace had opened his old wound. He'd had this week to think about Doll, and the more he'd thought, the less excuse he could see for her acting the way she had. He hadn't built a fine house as Cummings had, but he'd made a start, and it had been for Doll.

She was cheap and small, he thought savagely. He'd get the other forty dollars he needed, some way. He'd pay Abbot off and then he'd be where he wanted to be. Alone! And next winter his bed would be cold just as it had been for the past three winters.

He led the horses back to where Grace waited; he gave her a hand up into the saddle. He mounted, and they turned south along the willow-lined river. Clouds had rolled up into the sky, black and ominous, and the wind, coming in off the desert, smelled wet and tangy with sage.

"I was married once, Rod," Grace said. "Maybe you didn't know." He shook his head and she went on, "I thought George had told you. He knew all about it. Well, it didn't work. I was young and pig-headed and I went against Daddy's advice."

She glanced at him, her face shadowed by unhappy memory. He was silent, not knowing quite what was expected of him. He wondered why George hadn't told him. Not that it made any difference. But perhaps it had to George.

"Daddy says I'm like a hot-blooded mare," she said ruefully.

"I need someone who can hold a tight-rein on me. You know, a strong man." She laughed shakily. "The trouble is you don't find many men like that. I could have had George. I still can, but it wouldn't do. I told him so the other night."

So that was the way it was. George didn't have what, he wanted after all. Working for Karl Hermann wasn't enough, but it would have to do. He had taken the easy way; he gave the orders on Spade and he made good money and he didn't have to worry about bad weather and a slim calf crop. The loss would be Karl Hermann's.

But when winter came his bed would be as cold as Rod's; he could keep a straight face and pretend he had made the right choice when he had gone to work for Hermann, but now Rod knew how it was. No amount of pretending could cover up the fact that George was an unhappy man. Then Todd Shannon's unexplained visit began harrowing Rod's thoughts again. If Hermann was dead, Grace might be forced to turn to George.

Rod glanced up at the sky that was black and forbidding. Lightning slashed across it and thunder made a wicked rumble. He said, "We've got to go back."

She shivered as the wind struck at her. "It's too late, Rod. I've been stubborn and foolish, but it's no good now to say I'm sorry."

It was too late. The rain would come in a few minutes. Rod had never been here before, but he remembered Cummings telling about a line cabin he had built not far from here. Rod studied the long slope to his left. Nothing marred the bunch-grass except a few scattered junipers. Farther up deep gorges sliced into the side of the mountain, and rimrock was a black jagged line against the sky. They were in for it, he thought.

"George said there was a line cabin up here," Grace said uneasily. "Not far from a creek. He said there was grub and dry wood there."

"You know more about this country than I do," he said. "You didn't aim to find that line cabin, did you?"

She met his gaze blandly. "I just asked George in case something happened that we couldn't get back, and I guess it's happening. I wouldn't be afraid with you anyhow, Rod. You have a talent for shaping circumstances instead of letting circumstances shape you."

"You wouldn't be doing some shaping yourself, would you?"
"I might."
"Well, let's find that creek."

He touched the sorrel up, and within half a mile reached a

small, white-maned stream that chattered noisily as it pounded toward the river. "It's up there," Grace said "I can see it."

The first drops of rain hit them then. "Come on," Rod called, and swung up the creek. It would be touch and go, he thought, with the cabin a quarter of a mile away. Well, Grace couldn't complain. But probably she wouldn't anyhow.

She kept up with him, horses laboring on the grade. Rod glanced back. A black curtain of rain was moving across the valley toward them. They wouldn't make it, he thought, and they didn't. They were fifty yards from the cabin when it struck, hitting them with the violence of water thrown from a bucket. Within a few seconds they were soaked.

They pulled up in front of the cabin. "Go inside," Rod shouted above the racket of the storm. "I'll put the horses in the shed."

She slid out of the saddle and ran into the cabin. Rod rode on to the shed, leading Grace's mount. He took a moment to strip gear from the horses; he went outside and shut the shed door, then he sprinted toward the cabin, head down. He went in, smelling the musty odor of a place that had not been lived in for months.

When he closed the door, the light in the room was very thin. Grace was standing in the middle of the room, hugging her breasts and shivering. There was a candle on the table. Rod found a can partly filled with matches. He said, "Light the candle," and gave her a match. Juniper wood was piled along the wall.

Apparently it hadn't occurred to Grace to start a fire, he thought irritably. She hadn't even looked for matches. He got a fire going, and in a moment the crackle of it was a pleasant sound in the room. Grace remained by the table, watching him intently, the thin light of the candle on her face.

He looked at her, the irritation leaving him. She'd do. The average woman would be blaming him for her discomfort, but Grace was a long ways from being average. Rod had started this job hating her father and believing he would dislike her. Now, in spite of himself, he admired Karl Hermann. Grace? Well, he didn't know how he felt, but he had been dead wrong about her.

He was still looking at her when she began to unbutton her blouse. Rod turned back to the stove and held his hands out to it, giving her his back.

"This is a funny time to be modest," Grace said as if amused. "Take your clothes off, Rod. We'll get pneumonia if we don't."

"The cabin'll be warm in a few minutes . . ."

"And in a few minutes I'll have a chill if you don't get me warm." She dropped her blouse across a bench, and taking off her wet skirt, laid it on the blouse. She came to him and putting her hands on his arms, tugged gently at him.

"Rod," she said. "Rod."

He looked down at her face, still wet with the rain. Momentary panic was in him. She had planned it this way. If the storm hadn't come up, she would have found some other excuse to come to the cabin. Perhaps she would have been too tired to ride back. Or they might have gone on to the top of the mountain and it would have been dark when they came down and she would have said she was afraid to go back to Spade.

He said, "You're wet as a drowned rat." He pulled away from her and found a towel behind the stove. "You ought to take your hair down."

He gave her the towel and picking up a bucket, went out into the storm. He ran to the creek, and filling the bucket, returned to the cabin. Grace had taken off the rest of her clothes and was sitting on a bench by the stove, wrapped in a blanket. She looked at him, laughing softly.

"Rod, if you think I'm wet, you should look at yourself."

Water ran off him in little streams, and he left muddy tracks on the plank floor as he crossed the room to the stove. His clothes clung to him, and he was cold, although the stove was hot now. He shivered as he poured water into the coffee pot and put it on the front of the range.

"Rod, you crazy man," Grace said in exasperation. "I won't nurse you if you're sick in bed. There's just no sense to it. You'll find another blanket on the bunk. Take your clothes off and hang them by the stove."

"I'll be all right," he muttered, and finding a can of coffee on a shelf, took the lid off, and dribbled enough into the pot to make the coffee black and strong. "This'll take the hair off."

She was removing the pins from her hair, still smiling. "Don't make it so strong we can't sleep, Rod. I wouldn't take that ride back to Spade for anything and you can't leave me alone."

He put more wood into the fire box. She was right. He couldn't leave her. He didn't even want to. What a hell of a kink life had put in his twine. He had lost Doll and now he had Grace. But he was always one to look ahead and he knew this wouldn't work. Not over the long haul. Grace wouldn't like the Rocking R. She wouldn't live there with him.

He found two tin cups and brought them to the table. Coffee smell was filling the cabin, and when he glanced at Grace, she said, "I hope you're a good coffee maker. It smells awfully good."

Her hair lay down her back in a long, pale mass. She was still dabbing at it with a towel, still faintly smiling with the cool confidence of a woman who was used to having what she wanted. But he could not be sure whether she was thinking of just this day and this night, or the years ahead. Her father had been right in saying she was like a hot-blooded mare; that she needed someone who could hold a tight-rein on her. Well, he understood horses but he had no savvy about women. If he had, he wouldn't have lost Doll.

The thought of Doll filled him with sudden discontent. She had accused him of looking for bigger game. Well, why not? Grace had everything a man would want. He had heard married men complain about their wives, but Grace's husband would never have any reason to complain. He could be as sure of that as a man could ever be sure of anything about a woman. He had no reason to remain loyal to Doll. She had no strings on him now. She had cut them away herself, slashing with brutal strokes.

"Isn't that coffee done?" Grace asked.

"I reckon," he said, and lifting the coffee pot, carried it to the table and filled the cups.

When he took the pot back to the stove, she rose and came to him, one hand clutching the blanket tightly over her breasts. She breathed, "Rod, you're so strange, so far away."

Her face was upturned to his. He put his arms around her and kissed her. She clung to him, making no secret of her hunger and wanting him to know that his lips were not enough. Then she drew back, one hand caressing his cheek.

He told himself that the long haul didn't make any difference; it didn't make any difference whether she liked the Rocking R or not. There was this moment. She had stirred him with her kiss as she had known she could, and suddenly all restraint went out of him and he picked her up and carried her to the bunk.

The coffee in the tin cups on the table cooled. Outside the storm grew in intensity and the rain hammered against the cabin, but they did not hear it.

Chapter XIII

THE AFTERNOON was almost gone when Rod and Grace returned to Spade. The day had been warm and clear, and Grace had insisted on riding to the top of the mountain before they started back. Yesterday's storm had cleared away the haze which had blurred the buttes to the west; it had given the earth a clean, scented smell.

Grace, awed by the size and beauty of this country, had been reverently silent while she sat her saddle, eyes on the somber-hued desert that lay beyond the valley of the Bearclaw and ran on and on until it met the down-swinging arc of the sky. As they rode back to Spade, Rod thought about how Grace had sat there so long as if unable to fully satisfy the hunger that this country aroused in her.

It was a side of her that surprised him. She didn't mention it on the way to the ranch, but he was sure she wasn't pretending, that all the luxury and social position which Karl Hermann's money could buy had not fully compensated for this part of life which she had lacked.

The thought that had touched his mind the afternoon before was there again and left him vaguely uneasy. Grace would not be willing to share his dream and work and the inevitable hardships which were bound to go with the development of the Rocking R. Or even if she lived at Spade, she would in time tire of the slow-paced and often dreary life of the cattle country.

Then a restlessness was in him, and he thought bitterly that he had lost the only really important thing in his life when he had lost Doll. No woman, Grace or any other, would ever take Doll's place. He should have told Grace that.

He could not help comparing the two women. In many ways Doll was still immature, but in spite of her changeable and often violent moods, she had the characteristics that he wanted in a wife. But Grace was already a woman, pliant in some regards, doggedly stubborn in others. In the end the man she married would bow to her; he would become Mr. Grace Hermann.

The Spade buildings were in sight when Grace said, "You're being mysterious again today, Rod."

He stared straight ahead, remembering that he had perversely refused to tell her he loved her. The restlessness grew in him, rooted, perhaps, in a sense of guilt. He had not been entirely fair with Grace, and he realized that when a man lost one woman, he instinctively turned to another.

"No," he said finally. "I just ain't gabby."

"You've demonstrated that all week," she said tartly. "I've had to dig for everything, but now I've got my rope on you, or you've got yours on me, whichever way you want to say it."

It made a hell of a lot of difference to a man which way you said it, he thought. He forced himself to look at her; he saw the proud way she held her head, the little confident smile lingering at the corners of her mouth as if she had finally accomplished something she had set out to do.

"Grace, we might as well get this straight," he said. "I'm little fry, I always will be, and I don't want to be anything else."

"Oh, you're talking crazy," she said impatiently. "Nobody wants to be little when he can have the moon by reaching for it."

"I do," he said.

She was silent, apparently sensing that this was not the time to press the issue, and then suddenly he remembered what Karl Hermann had said the first day they had come to the valley. "She's always looking for men. She collects them." Hermann had been warning him, but at the time, he had not realized it.

They stopped in front of the house and Rod stepped down and gave her a hand. He saw Juan Herrara and Clay Cummings move toward them from the corral. He said, "There's Clay now, Grace."

"Why, he looks just like I thought he would," she said. "His wife was a fool. After all this time, he's not beaten."

"A man like him never gets beaten." When Cummings came up, Rod said, "Clay, meet Grace Hermann. She's an admirer of yours."

Cummings took off his hat and stared at Grace, his craggy face grave. "I reckon he's lying, ma'am. I'm an old horse put out on pasture, but nobody's got the guts it takes to shoot me."

She laughed and held out a slim hand. "I know horses, Mr. Cummings. I never saw a valuable horse get so old that he wasn't worth having around." She motioned toward the house. "You did a marvelous thing, coming here when you did. It wasn't fair for Daddy to take advantage of the work you did."

He took her hand, plainly surprised by what she said. Then he stepped back, still staring at her and frankly admiring her, a white-headed eagle of a man in whom the love of life was still a strong force.

"It wasn't a proposition of taking advantage, ma'am," he said. "Your dad was just a smart business man." He wheeled to Rod, jerking his head toward the bunkhouse. "Let Juan take care of the horses. I want to talk to you."

Cummings strode across the yard to the bunkhouse. Rod glanced at Grace who looked as if she had half a mind to follow him. Rod said, "I'll see you at supper."

She laughed softly. "There goes a man. You bring him in for supper."

Rod nodded and caught up with Cummings. "Just ride in, Clay?"

"Last night." Cummings gave him a reproving glance. "You and the girl were out lallygagging, looks like."

"We got caught in the storm," Rod said.

Cummings snorted. "Wasn't that big a storm, boy. Hell's fire, you lost your savvy?"

"No."

"Looks to me like you have. I didn't figure you were that soft in the head. Doll's your kind of woman, Rod. Take an old man's word for it who got run through a sausage grinder."

He was thinking of his wife, Rod thought. Cummings had been a wealthy man then, but it hadn't satisfied the woman he had picked. After he had lost her, he probably hadn't cared much what had happened to him.

They went into the bunkhouse. Rod sat down and rolled a smoke. Cummings paced around like a nervous mountain lion. Finally he said, "I'm poking my nose into business that ain't mine, but I'm poking it anyhow. Why you don't put a hole in Jason Abbot's skull is something I don't know."

"He hasn't given me a chance yet. He don't do his own fighting."

"Then run him out of the country," Cummings snapped. "He's a spider, a damned old spider working like hell on his web. He misfired that day you fetched the Hermanns to the valley, but he ain't done. He's cooking up something else, but I don't know what it is."

"He threw a little lead the other night. Hear about it?"

Cummings nodded. "Sure I heard. Hermann's so mad he can't spit, which same is what Abbot wanted. But there's something else. Abbot's crazy, Rod, plumb loco. He won't be satisfied till he gets you and Hermann, and Doll and Marcia are the ones who'll get hurt."

Rod finished his smoke and rolled another, sensing that the old man was having trouble saying what was in his mind. Cummings sat down and got up at once and began walking around the long room again.

"I saw you smoke Barney Webb down," Cummings said. "You done good. I figured you'd slowed up, but I reckon when a man learns to use a gun, he don't never forget." He waggled a long, gnarled finger at Rod. "But you're lucky to be alive. Know where Chuck England was?"

"No, but I've sure been wondering."

"Upstairs in the hotel. He was in a room facing the street, and he was gonna cut you down before you plugged Webb. Abbot had it all schemed out."

It tallied, Rod thought. He asked, "Well, why didn't he?"

"You chowder-headed idiot," Cummings shouted, "riding around with the Hermann girl and staying out all night with her. Hell's bells, you ain't got a lick of sense or you'd know why you're still alive."

"All right," Rod said irritably. "I'm an idiot. Now tell me why I'm alive."

"Because Doll took a shotgun and went upstairs and held it on England till you was out of town. That's why. I got it out of Marcia, and I guess there was hell to pay afterwards when Abbot saw her."

Rod stared at the floor, unable to say anything, unable even to think coherently. Doll who had cut everything off between them and accused him of wanting Grace had saved his life. She must love him. She wouldn't have done it if she hadn't.

Rod looked at Cummings, utterly miserable. "She gave me my walking papers, Clay. She was done with me."

Cummings threw up his hands. "What you don't know about women would sure fill a book. You gave her up mighty damned easy. If you really loved her, you'd . . ."

"All right," Rod said. "I'll go to town after supper."

Cummings laughed. "With Grace Hermann, I reckon."

Rod heard the triangle then, and rose. "You're eating in the house, Clay."

"I ain't doing no such thing."

"Grace's invitation. If you don't, she'll eat with you."

Cummings groaned. "To hell with stubborn women," he said, but he went.

Hermann and George were in the living room. They spoke to Rod, making no mention of the night before, but George was glum, silent and withdrawn, and Rod sensed the deep anger that was in his brother. But Hermann was as friendly as ever. He would not, Rod thought, be shocked by anything Grace did.

After they had finished eating, Hermann leaned back in his chair and lighted a cigar. He said, "Clay, I need you. George won't let me leave Spade to see these fool settlers. Says it's dangerous."

"He's right," Cummings said, "which same you oughtta know after getting your windows shot out."

"Rod says that was just Abbot." Hermann pounded on the table, furious again as he thought about the attack. "I'm going to see that ornery son hang before I leave here, but I was thinking about the others. If I could talk to them, maybe I could convince them I didn't come here to make trouble, though I'm not sure it was just Abbot."

Cummings shook his head. "I'll go see 'em, if that's what you want. Won't do no good, though."

"Might," Rod said. "Looks to me like Abbot don't have 'em eating out of his hand like he did, or they'd have been with him the other night." He glanced at George, wondering again about Todd Shannon, then he added, "It's my guess Abbot had England and Shannon with him the other night."

But George's somber expression was not altered by Rod's words. Hermann said, "The other night I was mad enough to call the crew in and clean out the north side of the valley, but I've never done anything like that and I won't now. Not till I hear what luck you have, Clay." He rose. "Rod, I want to talk to you in the office."

Hermann left the room. Rod's gaze touched Grace's face. She was smiling, a cool, confident smile that showed what was in her mind as clearly as spoken words. Rod left the dining room, a little uneasy about this. When he reached the office, he saw that Hermann was sitting behind the desk, the swivel chair canted back.

"Sit down, Rod," Hermann said. "I'm not a man to beat around the bush. I'll admit I was wrong about you when I first got here. Since there is no law in this valley, and with this fellow Abbot kicking up a dust, why, I guess I need men of your caliber."

"You didn't bring me here to say that."

Hermann laughed. "You're right. I was going to say there was a time when I thought Grace and George would make a go of it. That suited me fine because George is the kind of man I'd like for a son-in-law, but it won't work." He eased his chair down and leaned forward. "The reason is Grace has taken a shine to you."

"I don't . . ."

"Wait till I get done talking," Hermann interrupted. "Grace winds me around her finger. I don't try to figure out why she wants what she wants. I just work like hell to get it for her. She wants you. If she hadn't made that plain, I will."

Rod stared at Hermann, thinking that this was the first time since he had met Karl Hermann that the man was talking like a million dollars. He had been in the habit of buying anything Grace wanted, and it had not occurred to him that Rod Devers could not be bought.

He should be mad enough to kick a few teeth down Hermann's throat, but for some reason he wasn't. He said, "You told me Grace collected men."

"That's the funny part of it," Hermann said. "This time she's serious. Now I'm a business man, Rod. One thing I've learned is that if you don't grab what you want when you have a chance, you won't get anything when you do grab. This notion you've got of owning a spread is crazy. I'm offering you a free ticket for anywhere you want to go."

"You've got the wrong man," Rod said.

"Wait a minute," Hermann shouted, affronted by a turndown as cold as this. "You're the right man for Grace. I saw that the day we were in Poplar City. You've got a lot of the qualities I had when I was young and full of vinegar. You're tough enough to take my job over." He frowned, his eyes on Rod's bleak face, then asked, "It's not on account of your father and what my bank did, is it? I didn't know anything about that deal till it was wound up."

"No, I've changed my mind about you," Rod said. "It just wouldn't work out. I can't take your ticket and Grace wouldn't live my way. I . . ."

Someone was pounding on the front door. Rod heard George say, "Come in," and then Doll's voice, "Is Rod here?"

Chapter XIV

As long as Doll lived, she would never forget those terrible moments when she stood in the hotel room overlooking the street, the cocked shotgun in her hands lined on Chuck England. She had backed him into a corner and then had moved to the window, trying to watch him and see what was going on in the street at the same time.

She was scared, thoroughly and completely scared, and she was trembling so much that her finger began pressing against the trigger before she realized it. England was even more frightened than she was, but for a different reason. His pallid face showed that he knew no one was more dangerous than a scared woman with a gun in her hands.

"Ease up," he called to her several times. "I ain't gonna jump you."

Each time her finger relaxed and then, before she knew what she was doing, her finger began to tighten again. But she never pulled the trigger. England's words kept her from it.

She had never seen Rod draw a gun. She had never seen a gun fight. She had never seen a man die. She saw all of those things that afternoon, and unconsciously she breathed a prayer for Rod when he stood facing Barney Webb.

Later, a long time later, it seemed to her, she let England go after Rod had ridden out of town. She said, "You'd better leave the valley, England."

He had given her a wicked look. "You're the one who had best leave, ma'am. What do you think Abbot's gonna do when he hears about this?"

She didn't care, now that Rod was safe. She ran to her room, not thinking until afterwards that she had let England keep his gun and that he could have shot her in the back. She dropped the shotgun and throwing herself on the bed, began to cry from sheer relief.

It had been more or less an accident that she had been able to do what she had. She and her mother had been watching from the room Rod had occupied. They had not known England was in the next room until they heard someone moving around, and when Webb appeared in the street, Marcia whispered, "Doll, I know what Jason meant when he said England was his ace in the hole. England's in the next room and he'll shoot Rod in the back."

Doll remembered the shotgun in her room and she ran down the hall to get it. She picked it up and went back and opened the door of England's room. He was facing the window, so it was easier than she had thought it would be. She'd said. "Get over into the corner," and he'd obeyed.

She laughed suddenly, remembering the expression on England's face when he'd turned around, a high sound that shocked her because she had not realized how close she was to hysteria. She laughed again, wondering how England had explained his failure to Abbot.

She dropped off to sleep, worn out by those few moments of nervous tension while she had held England in the corner. Late in the afternoon her mother called her. She went downstairs to wait on tables, but the instant the dining room cleared out, she stepped into the lobby. She had never understood why her mother hated Hermann and she had been afraid to ask, but now she had to know.

"You've got to tell me about Hermann," Doll said, "because it seems to me you're foolish to let something that happened a long time ago . . ."

"I am foolish," Marcia said. "I didn't realize how foolish until a few days ago." She rose. "Let's go back to the parlor."

They went along the hall, Marcia in front, and suddenly Doll wished she hadn't asked. It had been a secret kept for so many years, and there was no good reason for it to be told now. But when they were in the parlor and she said, "You don't have to . . ." Marcia made a quick, silencing gesture.

"I want to tell you." Marcia picked up her embroidery and sat down in her rocking chair. "But before I do, I . . ." She paused, head bending over her embroidery. "I love you, Doll. Nothing else is important."

Shocked, Doll stared at her mother. Love had never been a subject for talk between them, but she had not doubted her mother's love, and she saw no reason why she should be assured of it now. For a moment she watched Marcia's right hand move with feverish speed, pushing the needle through the taut cloth and pulling the blue thread tight, and then she realized her mother was waiting.

Doll cried out, "I know you love me. I never said anything . . ."

"No." Marcia glanced up and then went on sewing. "The trouble is I haven't lived the kind of life you could be proud of. By most people's standards, I'm a bad woman. I'm sorry, Doll, but I can't undo what I've done."

"No one ever had a better mother," Doll whispered.

Marcia smiled. "It makes me happy to hear that. I'm taking a long way around to say what I want to say. A woman has to be wise about a man if she's going to be happy, and you haven't been very smart with Rod. What you said at noon . . ."

"I know," Doll said. "I love him so much I'm not good for him. When Abbot said what he did . . ." She stopped, thinking Rod must hate her. He had every right to. "I don't suppose I'll ever have a chance to tell him I'm sorry."

"I have an idea you will." Marcia went on sewing, her eyes on the cloth. "You wanted to know about Hermann. It isn't a nice story. I lived with him for a few months when I was very young. I thought he was going to marry me, but he met another woman he liked better, and I never found another man I could love."

Marcia laid her embroidery on the table. "Sometimes love and hate are very close, Doll. I've been as foolish hating Hermann as you have in loving Rod and demanding so much of him." She took a long breath. "Well, there's nothing to do now but wait. When the time comes, we'll stop Jason, somehow."

"You'll never stop me."

Doll whirled to face the door. Jason Abbot stood there, glaring at Marcia, his green eyes filled with the wickedness of an angry cat. Doll had no way of knowing how long he had been there, or how much he had heard.

"Get out," Doll screamed. "Don't ever come back."

Marcia was on her feet facing Abbot. She laid a hand on Doll's arm. "Let him talk," she said. "He always gives himself away when he talks."

"Not this time," Abbot said, "but I'll tell you one thing. I haven't played my top cards. When I do, I'll bring Devers to town where I can get at him, and then I'll get Hermann. That's what you wanted, Marcia. Or have you forgotten?"

Marcia ignored the question. She asked, "And just how will you bring Rod to town?"

"You'll see." He turned his eyes to Doll. "You're going to marry me. Right now you're sure you never will, but someday you'll feel different."

"I wouldn't marry . . ."

"All right, all right," Abbot cut in, "but any woman can change her mind. Now leave me and your mother alone."

"I wouldn't leave her with you," Doll cried.

"Don't worry," Marcia said. "I've handled better men than him."

"I doubt that." Abbot smiled, the familiar air of superiority returning to him. "I've been all the man you ever wanted."

Doll looked at her mother, thinking this was wrong, but she left when Marcia motioned for her to go. She waited in the lobby, uneasy until Abbot went out through the back door a few minutes later. When she returned to the parlor, she saw that her mother was more composed than she had been.

"He just dressed me down for letting you save Rod's life," Marcia said. "You go on to bed. Nothing will happen for a few days."

Doll obeyed, sensing that her mother did not need her. She had a feeling that Abbot had told more than he had intended. Her mother would do what had to be done when the time came, although she wasn't sure Rod would ever need help again. She undressed and went to bed, her thoughts lingering on Rod. She wondered what she would say and what he would do the next time she saw him.

Then a new thought came to her, shocking her and bringing her upright in bed. She had never known her father. Her mother had told her he had died before she was born, but now she wondered if he was Karl Hermann.

For a long time she sat there, staring at the black wall in front of her, her mind numb as if a great weight were pressing against her head. She whispered, "God, don't let it be that way."

She could not blot the thought from her mind during the following, frenzied days of waiting. She worried constantly about Rod. She heard nothing from Spade; she did not see Abbot or England, and even Sam Kane and Otto Larkin and their neighbors stayed away from town.

Everyone seemed to be involved in a conspiracy of silence, then it broke one afternoon while she was helping Ada in the dining room. Her mother had gone to the store to buy groceries. She appeared in the lobby door, her face pale and harried, and motioned for Doll to come to her.

"Todd Shannon was in the store," Marcia whispered when Doll stood beside her. "He was shooting off his mouth the way he does when he's a little drunk. One of us has got to ride to Spade to see Rod. There's no one else we can trust. If you don't want to go, I will."

"Of course I'll go," Doll said. "What do you want me to tell him?"

Chapter XV

For a moment Rod stood there at Hermann's desk, unable to believe it was Doll's voice he had heard, then he wheeled and went through the door. Doll was standing on the porch, the light from the living room falling across her face. In his first glance Rod saw that something was wrong. He had never seen her look this way before, pale and worried and thoroughly scared. Then she saw Rod and brushing past George, ran to him.

He was going to thank her for saving his life; he wanted most of all to tell her he hadn't known how it was until an hour or two ago, but he didn't have a chance to say anything. Words poured out of her in an almost incoherent stream.

"They say you've been rustling calves and the 99 is going to burn you out and hang you if they catch you."

He caught her hands, surprised when he felt how cold they were. "Where'd you hear that?"

"Ma heard Todd Shannon talking about it in the store. I guess he was pretty drunk. He said you'd run as soon as you heard about it."

Rod glanced at George. He murmured, "Todd Shannon, was it?" but his brother's somber expression told him nothing.

"You know how he is when he's been drinking," Doll said. "Talks so big and tough when he isn't that way at all."

"I know," Rod said, still looking at George.

"What are you going to do?" George asked.

"I'm not worried about 'em getting me for rustling because I didn't steal any calves," Rod answered, "but they may burn me out. Looks like I'd better go home."

"You can't go by yourself," Doll cried. "That's what they want."

"Sure," Rod said. "Abbot put Shannon up to his gabbing in front of your ma, knowing you'd get word to me, so I'll oblige him."

"Don't go alone," Doll said. "Ask your brother for help."

106

"Rod."

It was Grace's voice, peremptory and commanding. When he turned to her, he saw an expression of incredible shock on her face as if she could not believe she was seeing him hold another woman's hands.

"This is Doll Nance," Rod said. "Doll, I want you to meet Grace Hermann."

George and Cummings were standing there, embarrassed and uneasy. Doll said, "How do you do?" But Grace made no pretense of greeting Doll. She walked toward Rod, her head held high.

"I don't know what this is all about," Grace said in a shrewish tone, "but this girl had better leave."

"I'm going to," Doll said, turning toward the door.

"I'm going with her," Rod said. "I've got a hunch this is what we've been waiting for."

"You're not going," Grace snapped. "You've got a job to do and it's here."

"That's right," George said. "You can't walk out . . ."

"Hermann said I'd better be earning my wages," Rod said, "and that's what I aim to do."

Rod started toward the door when he heard Hermann call, "Wait." He swung around. Hermann stood in the doorway of the office staring at Doll, his face as gray as weathered wood. He brought a hand up to clutch his throat. He whispered, "Marcia," and then his knees buckled and he fell forward on his face.

Grace screamed. George was the first to reach Hermann. He knelt and felt of his pulse. He said, "He's fainted. Let's get him over to the couch, Rod."

They carried him to the leather couch, Grace crying, "It's his heart."

"I can't help him," Rod said. "I might as well be riding."

He strode out of the house, ignoring Grace's scream, "Rod, you can't go. I won't let you."

He crossed to the corrals; he caught and saddled his sorrel, and when he stepped up, he saw that Grace was standing a few feet from him, her face haggard in the thin dusk light. He said, "I'm sorry about your dad. I hope he'll be all right."

"It's you I'm thinking about," Grace said, "not him. Don't I mean anything to you?"

He looked down at her, knowing that he would never love her. Even if he did, he could not change his attitude about going to work for Karl Hermann, and she would never change hers about being a small cowman's wife.

"It wouldn't do," he said. "I told your dad tonight."

There was no trace of the cool confidence which usually dominated her. Motioning toward Doll who had mounted and was waiting by the poplars, she said in a hurt tone, "It's her, isn't it?"

"No," Rod said. "You'n me just couldn't make a go of it."

He rode away, leaving her staring after him. When Doll caught up with him, he asked, "Why did Hermann call you Marcia?"

Doll was silent until they crossed the bridge spanning Half-mile Creek, then she said, "How should I know?"

Well, maybe she didn't. He said, "Clay told me you saved my life when I had the fight with Webb. Thanks."

"I couldn't let him kill you."

He was unable to tell anything from her voice. He was silent, deciding that nothing had changed between them. Later, when they reached the edge of town, Doll said, "Put my horse in the stable and fetch Ma's mare back to the hotel. I'm going with you."

He had not expected that. If he was guessing right, and he was sure he was, Abbot had baited a trap to lure him back to the Rocking R and then Abbot would move in on him with England and Shannon. Rod discounted Shannon as a fighting man, but it was still long odds, even against Abbot and England.

If he had guessed wrong and Kane and his neighbors showed up with Abbot, Rod Devers was a dead man if they caught him alone on the Rocking R. But he had thought about that possibility before he left Spade and decided it was a risk he had to take. Either way, there would be a fight, so Doll would have to stay in town.

"No," Rod said. "You're staying here."

"You can't keep me from going," she flared. "I never dreamed you'd do a crazy thing like riding out there alone, or I wouldn't have gone to Spade. I thought you'd bring some of the Spade hands and be ready for Abbot."

"I couldn't ask George for help," Rod said.

"I suppose that's more of your pride again," she cried.

"No. It's just that Hermann has some strong ideas about cowhands working at their business. Anyhow, there wasn't anyone at Spade. Just a blacksmith and one of Clay's old vaqueros who's too bunged up to ride."

"If you go alone, you'll be killed. "Don't you see, Rod? I'd blame myself as long as I lived."

"You've got no cause for that," he said. "Fighting used to be my trade. I figure I'm still pretty good at it."

"Of course you are. That's all the more reason for me to go with you. I'd be safe."

That was female reasoning, he thought ruefully. He said, "No, you're staying in town."

"I'm going," she said doggedly.

He let it go for the moment. They rode down Main Street, deserted and ominously quiet. Brief doubt touched Rod. The trap might be laid here. Instinctively his eyes searched the dark street and the gaps between the buildings, but there was no hint of movement. He was just jumpy, he thought, and decided that nothing would happen here. The trouble would be at the Rocking R where there would be no friendly witnesses to his death.

They reined up in front of the hotel, the light from the lobby touching Doll's face. Rod looked at her, seeing the stubborn expression that was so familiar to him. This was another clash of wills, he thought, and then he realized she was certain she was right about going just as he was certain he was right about her staying in town.

Because his growing anger was tempered by that knowledge, he said gently, "Fighting is a man's job, Doll. If you got killed and I lived, I'd blame myself, too, you know."

She turned her head so he could not see her face. "I'll put my horse away, Rod. Ma wants to see you before you leave town."

"I haven't got time . . ."

"It won't take you more than a minute," she broke in. "You owe her that much."

A man never completely escaped from the obligations he owed other people, Rod thought. His only motive in taking the job George had offered was a selfish one, but once he had accepted and taken his pay, he had placed himself in a position where he was bound to the Hermanns until this trouble was settled.

He didn't owe George anything. Still, he was trapped by the fact that George was his brother. It was the only reason he had not forced George to explain Todd Shannon's presence at Spade that evening. Not a good reason, perhaps, but it had restrained him because he didn't want George to know he distrusted him until he had more to go on than mere suspicion and Sam Kane's prejudiced hunch.

But for Doll to say he owed her mother anything was piling it on. He started to tell her so when he remembered Doll had saved his life. His debt was to her, not Marcia, but if she wanted him to see her mother, he would do it for her.

"All right," he said, and dismounting, looped the reins around the hitch pole.

Doll rode on down the street toward the stable without a backward glance. For a moment Rod stood watching her, not sure what she was going to do. He had not convinced her, but there was nothing more he could say.

When he went into the hotel, he saw that Marcia was not in the lobby. She must have heard him come in, for she called from her parlor, "That you, Rod?"

"Yeah, it's me." He waited at the desk until she came down the hall, and when he saw her, he said, "Doll's got a notion she wants to go with me tonight. It's too dangerous. You make her stay here."

Marcia was as pale as she had been the day the Hermanns had come to the valley. But there was something else about her that bothered him, something that gave him the feeling she was a stranger. She looked as if she had forgotten how to laugh, as if she had lived under the shadow of an overpowering worry every day since Rod had seen her.

"Let her go with you, Rod," Marcia said wearily. "And keep on going. Don't stop at the Rocking R."

He gripped her arms. "Do you know anything about this business I don't know?"

She shook her head, utterly miserable. "Jason doesn't confide in me any more. But I know him, Rod. You've got to get out of the valley. What's happened is just the beginning."

She jerked free of his grip and stepping behind the desk, picked up a small sack that was filled with gold coins. "This is all I have, Rod. Take Doll and leave the valley."

She held the sack out to him. He took it and set it on the desk. "You ain't telling me all you know, Marcia."

"I don't know anything else," she cried, "except one thing you won't admit. You can't fight everybody. That's why I want Doll to go with you before you're killed. For God's sake, take her if you love her."

She said it imploringly as if it were a prayer. Rod knew from the terrible fear shadowing her face that it was Doll's future she worried about and this was the only thing she could do for her daughter.

He shook his head, convinced Doll would not go away with him even if he asked her. Going with him to the Rocking R to help him fight was one thing, but leaving the valley and her mother was something else.

"I figure Doll's finished with me," he said. "Anyhow, I gave my word to George. I can't leave until I've done the job he hired me for."

He wheeled toward the door. Marcia screamed, "Rod," and running to him, grabbed his arm and turned him to face her. "Rod, listen to me. We've hated Hermann for years, but that isn't important to either one of us now. Doll's safety is. This isn't your fight and it isn't hers. If you stay, you'll both get hurt. That's why I sent Doll to Spade. Get her out of the valley before it's too late."

"Why do you hate Hermann?"

She looked away. "I can't tell you."

"He saw Doll tonight. He called her Marcia."

For a moment he thought she was going to faint. She put a hand to her head and moved back to the desk and leaned against it. She said, "I don't know why he'd do a crazy thing like that."

"I think you do. You ought to tell me."

She shook her head. "I can't. I'm not proud of myself, Rod. I've rolled in the mud until I'm covered with it, but the mud hasn't touched Doll. I love her, Rod. I want to know she's taken care of, and you're the only man who can."

"Doll will make out," he said gently.

He left the lobby, hearing her crying softly, and he was surprised. He had always thought she was a woman who would never give way to her feelings. But she was not the Marcia Nance he had known. Something out of her past had returned to plague her when Hermann had come to the valley, something she was too ashamed to tell him. It was changing her, and breaking her.

Chapter XVI

ROD LEFT TOWN at a gallop, relieved when he was out on the grass and the lights of Poplar City were behind him. He pulled up after he had gone a mile or so, and sat listening, afraid that Doll would follow him. But he heard nothing, and presently he went on, deciding that for once, she was going to do what he told her.

He rode northwest, following the creek, a thin moon hanging above the eastern rim of the valley, and presently he began to climb as he reached the northern slope that tipped up toward the foothills. He thought of Shannon's accusation that he had rustled his neighbors' calves, a charge so fantastic that only a sick mind like Jason Abbot's would ever have thought about it.

Kane and Larkin and the others wouldn't give it a second thought. They knew him too well. At least he wanted to think they did. But he had beaten Kane that night in the Palace, and Kane was a stubborn man who would hold it against him. There was a chance Abbot had framed him by slapping the Rocking R on a few calves, and Kane, humiliated as he had been, might accept the evidence without question.

He had not considered this possibility before and now it began to bother him. Maybe they had already burned him out and scattered his cattle from hell to breakfast. If they had gone that far, they would certainly be waiting up here for him. They'd be afraid to let him live.

He shook his head, telling himself he was as jumpy as he had been when he'd ridden into town with Doll. His first guess was right. Abbot didn't have the backing of the north valley men, or they'd have been with him when they'd made the attack on Spade.

The mountains lifted directly ahead of him, pine-covered and black against the star-speckled sky. The country was tilting more sharply now, and presently he made out the vague shape of his cabin and sheds in front of him. At least he hadn't been burned out.

He reined up and sat listening, but he heard nothing except

the hooting of an owl far back in the timber. They might be here, in the cabin or one of the sheds, or outside the cabin, pressing against the wall so they'd be lost in the night shadows, waiting for him to come close.

He swore softly, knowing he had to make sure about this. He couldn't stay here all night. It seemed a fair guess that he had got here ahead of them. Abbot had no way of knowing when he would come. If Abbot and his men thought he'd wait until morning, they might not show up until later in the night, or sometime tomorrow.

Stepping down, he sprinted toward the cabin, gun in his hand. Still no sound. He felt a prickle run down his spine that stemmed from a natural fear of the unknown. Gunflame might blossom from the darkness at any moment, but it was a risk he was purposely taking because he no longer had any capacity for waiting.

He reached the front door of his cabin and shoved it open, standing to one side so he wouldn't be silhouetted against the moonlight. The door made a rump-tingling squeal in the pressing silence, loud enough to warn anyone who was reasonably close. Not that it made any difference. If they were here, they'd have seen him before now and they'd have cut him down. He shook his head, deciding he'd better make sure. Jason Abbot was not a man who would follow the usual pattern.

He slid through the door, gun still palmed, and put his back to the wall. It was black dark except for the faint splash of light coming through the open door and windows. He made a quick search of the room, certain now he had beaten them here, and then it occurred to him that he had never, during the years when he had hired his gun, taken as foolish a chance with his life as he had just now.

The difference lay in the fact that a man looks at danger one way when he's hired to risk his life, and in quite another when his own property is the stake. He had lived here for three years; he had dreamed his dreams about sharing the cabin with Doll, so it meant something that no other place would ever mean. Now, going back across the yard for his horse, he felt the sharp letdown that naturally followed the relief of finding everything all right.

He stripped gear from his sorrel and let the horse into the corral, then he returned to the cabin. He shut and barred the door, wondering if he could sleep. No one could get in without waking him, and he felt the bone-deep weariness of the long ride. It was probably more nervous than physical, for waiting and uncertainty took more out of a man than riding would ever take.

No use even to try to sleep, he decided, and knew it would be worse before morning with more waiting and more uncertainty. He considered the possibility that Abbot had planned this to worry him, then discounted the thought at once. Jason Abbot was probably more nervous than he was. For all of his scheming, he had been unable to bring this to a head. No, they'd come, tomorrow if not tonight.

They! How often that word had been in his mind. They'd come, but who would it be? Kane? Larkin? All of them, fifteen or more? No, it would just be Abbot and England and Shannon. He swore savagely, and going back to the door, lifted the bar, and opened it. He stood there, staring into the night. He had gone over this time after time, assuring himself he was right, but still there was this doubt. If he had figured it wrong, he'd made a fatal mistake holing up this way in his cabin.

He stiffened. Someone was coming. At first he thought it was just his imagination, his taut nerves playing tricks with his hearing. Then he knew there was no doubt about it. From the steady drum of hoofs, he judged it was just one horse, coming fast, and not far away.

He drew his gun, puzzled by this. England, maybe. Neither Abbot nor Shannon would have enough courage to come in alone. But it might be a trick designed to pull him into the open while the other two worked downslope through the timber north of the cabin.

Close now, close enough to see the horse and rider. He pronged back the hammer of his gun. Stupid, he thought, just plain stupid, riding in this way. He raised the gun, but he held his fire, wondering how close the rider would come, then he heard his name called.

Doll! He eased the hammer down, a ragged breath breaking out of him as he sagged against the door jamb. He shouted, "Here, Doll." Of all the damn fool things she had ever done, this took top prize.

She reached the cabin and swung down as he moved toward her. She cried, "Are you all right?"

He put his arms around her and could not say anything for a moment. He wanted to shake her; he wanted to turn her over his knees and paddle her. But he did not do either. He said, his voice shaky, "You idiot, you crazy little idiot. Don't you know I might have shot you?"

"But you didn't," she said calmly. "Rod, some men have

been behind me. I couldn't tell how many, three or four. They chased me about two miles, then they swung off to the west and I lost them."

"Get inside." He gave her a push toward the door. "I'll put your horse up."

He led her lathered mount to the corral and stripped gear from her. It was Marcia's mare. Doll had changed in town, knowing her own horse was tired. If she hadn't, they probably would have caught up with her and shot her before they found out who she was.

He let the mare into the corral and shut the gate, then stood listening, sensing they were not far away. Again he wondered if it was his imagination. He didn't think so. More than once when he had fought for money, this strange warning feeling which he had never been able to define had saved his life.

He started across the yard toward the cabin. The instant he was away from the cover of the corral, three guns opened up from the tall grass of his meadow. He ran, bending low, bullets filling the air with the ugly whisper of their passage. One slapped through the crown of his Stetson, another drove through the back of his coat, burning his shoulder blades with white heat.

Doll had found his Winchester and now she cut loose from a window. By the time he reached the door, the firing from the grass had stopped. He plunged inside, slammed the door shut, and dropped the bar. He leaned against it, panting.

"You aren't hit?" Doll called from where she stood at the window.

"My hat's got a hole in it," he said, not mentioning the slug that had barely opened the skin along his back.

"You were lucky," she said in a matter-of-fact voice. "Took you a long time to put Ma's mare up. Took me a long time to find your rifle, too, feeling around in the dark."

He went to her. There was no firing now, and in the thin light washing through the window, he saw her face, as serene and composed as if this were an ordinary event she was used to. She had knocked the glass from the window and stood peering through it, waiting for a flash of gunfire to give her a target.

"Doll, I told you to stay in town."

"Why, I guess you did," she said, "but I had a talk with Ma. I'm a pretty good shot, Rod, so we decided this was where I belonged."

No sense in arguing about it now that she was here and

bottled up with him. He asked, "Know what we're in for?"

"A siege," she said. "How are we fixed on ammunition, grub, and water?"

"Plenty of shells and food." He hadn't thought about water. He could have filled a bucket from the small stream that flowed from the spring above the cabin. He added, "No water. My fault."

"I guess we can hold them off for awhile," she said. "If I know Abbot, he'll keep his distance."

The firing broke out again, closer this time. Rod moved to the other window. One man was still in the meadow, but the other two had taken cover in the horse shed. That was on the blind west side of the cabin, the bullets burying themselves in the thick pine logs.

Rod emptied his six-gun at the man in the grass, Doll banging away with the Winchester. Whoever was down there must have found some sort of cover, probably the irrigation ditch which was dry now. He fired at irregular intervals, and neither Rod nor Doll was able to silence him.

After a few minutes, the shooting stopped again. Rod was relieved on one point at least. There were only three of them, so he was sure it was Abbot and his men. He had guessed right.

The silence ran on for a time, and presently Doll asked, "What do you suppose they'll do?"

"Starve us out," Rod said. "I've got a hunch Abbot is wondering who's with me."

Doll laughed. "I'll bet he is. They probably thought they were chasing you. Judging by the direction they came from, they'd been out to Abbot's ranch. You probably got here sooner than they expected."

"I figured that after I didn't find 'em here," he said.

"If it was a little darker, we could go out after them," she said.

"We're staying inside." He paused, then asked, "Know anything about Kane and Larkin and their bunch?"

"Haven't heard a thing. They haven't been in town since the day the Hermanns came to the valley. Ma thinks they lost their nerve after you shot Webb."

Again the silence ran on, the minutes piling up. Rod tried to put himself in Abbot's place, wondering what the man would do. If it were later in the summer and the grass was dry, they might try to burn the cabin. That wouldn't work now, but one of them might bring trash from the shed and pile it on one of the blind sides of the cabin and fire it.

The possibility made Rod uneasy. He got a butcher knife and started working on the chinking on the west wall. He said, "I should have made some loopholes when I built the cabin, but I didn't think I'd ever be in this jam."

"Rod, there's something I've got to tell you," Doll said.

He went on digging between the logs. When she didn't go on, he asked, "Well?"

"I should have told you a long time ago," she said, "but I couldn't. Ma's to blame for this."

He yanked the knife blade back from the hole he had dug. He shouted, "What are you talking about?"

"When Hermann bought Spade," she said, "Ma knew that sooner or later he'd come here. She wanted to break him, kill him, anything to get even, so she started telling Abbot what a great man he was. She said he'd be as great as Hermann if he had the valley, and he believed her. That's why he's done the things he has."

"But Abbot's after my hide," Rod said, and went back to work with the knife.

"He figures he can't get Hermann until he gets you. Oh, I don't know, Rod. He's kind of crazy and he's got so many schemes. But it all started because Ma hated Hermann. She used to be his girl. She expected him to marry her, but he found someone else. I guess it's natural enough she'd hate him."

The thought had occurred to Rod many times that Doll would look like her mother when she got older. It must have worked the other way, too. Doll looked like Marcia when she was a girl, and Hermann, not knowing she was here in the valley, had been hit hard by the resemblance. In his mind he must have rolled back the years and thought he was seeing Marcia.

"I guess that explains Hermann fainting," Rod said. "Maybe he's still got her on his conscience."

He had dug through between the logs. Now he tossed the knife on the floor and peered through the hole. He could see the horse shed, but for a time there seemed to be no movement anywhere in the yard. He swore softly, thinking he'd have to do the same with the north wall. Fire was the only weapon Abbot could use to force them out of the cabin, and he would certainly think of it.

Rod started to draw back when he caught something moving just at the edge of his area of vision. He studied it a moment, not sure what he saw, for the moonlight was thin and deceptive. He only half heard Doll say, "There was something else

I didn't tell you awhile ago, Rod. About why I came. I think that if two people love each other, they should face every danger together. I couldn't stay away. Don't you see?"

The man in the hay meadow began firing again, and a moment later a rifle cut loose from the horse shed. Doll turned back to the window and opened with her Winchester. Rod, still watching the movement out there in the yard, finally made it out. A man was crawling toward the house shoving something in front of him.

Rod drew his gun and pushing the barrel through the hole, threw a shot at the crawling man. He missed, and fired again, and this time he scored. The man let out a squall of pain and jumping up, sprinted back toward the barn. Rod emptied his gun, but a moving man in light as thin as this was a poor target, and he was sure he missed.

The firing stopped again. Doll put down her rifle, asking, "What happened out there?"

Rod told her, and picking up the butcher knife, moved to the north wall and began hacking between the logs. He had no idea of time, but when he finished, the first gray trace of dawn was showing in the east. They'd try again, he thought, and wondered if Abbot would stay here all day, waiting for darkness to cover another attempt to burn the cabin.

As he worked, he kept thinking of what Doll had said. She did not repeat it. She probably wasn't sure he'd heard. For the first time, he began to doubt his own judgment about postponing their marriage. Doll had made no demands when she had come to help him tonight. She wanted to be with him. That was all.

He threw down his knife again and looked through the hole he had dug. For a long time he watched, a rosy prelude to sunrise showing along the eastern horizon, but he could not catch any hint of movement. He returned to the west wall and looked out. Doll was still at the window. Now she cried out, "Someone's coming, Rod. Maybe more than one. I can't tell."

He wheeled and ran to the window. She was right. Horses were coming in from the east. Kane, maybe. And Larkin. Perhaps more. He pulled her away from the window and looked at her and thought of all the things he should have said and wanted to say and hadn't. Maybe she was right about his pride. It was too late now to say anything except, "We're in trouble, Doll. I wish you weren't here."

She shook her head, smiling a little. "I wouldn't be anywhere else, Rod."

Chapter XVII

Rod RAN to the shelf that held his ammunition, wondering if Abbot would rush the cabin as soon as the new men got here. He threw a box of .30-.30 shells to Doll, then filled the empty loops of his cartridge belt. When he turned to Doll again, he saw that she was standing with her head tipped to one side as if listening, her body stiff with tension.

"What is it?" Rod asked.

"Abbot's leaving," she cried. "I'm sure of it. I can hear . . ."

Rod didn't wait for her to finish. He wheeled to the door and lifting the bar, yanked the door open. The morning light was still thin, but it was strong enough to make out three riders beyond the hay meadow. They were heading south on the run, apparently interested only in getting away.

Rod snatched the Winchester from Doll's hands, and taking rest against the door jamb, squeezed off five shots. As the smoke drifted away, he saw he had accomplished nothing except to hurry the three riders on their way. A moment later they were out of sight.

"These men that are coming . . ." Doll swallowed. "Rod, Abbot wouldn't pull out if he was getting help."

"He sure wouldn't," Rod agreed. "I didn't think we might be getting help instead of Abbot."

The men coming in from the east had swung north of the cabin into the timber. Now Clay Cummings' great voice came to Rod, "That you down there, Rod?"

"Clay! What do you know about that?" Rod ran to the corner of the cabin and waved his hat. "Sure it's me. Come on down."

A moment later Cummings came into sight and rode downslope toward the cabin. Another man followed him. Rod didn't recognize him for a moment, then he identified the bulky figure. Sam Kane!

Rod waited at the corner of the cabin until they reached him, Cummings calling, "What was all the shooting about?"

119

Rod kept his eyes on Kane whose face was still crusted with dark scabs from the fight they'd had in the Palace. He would not have been surprised if Kane had showed up to help Abbot, but for Kane to be with Cummings and for Abbot to clear out as he had just didn't make any sense.

"What was the shooting about?" Cummings asked, irritated by Rod's silence.

"I reckon you know without asking," Rod snapped. "Abbot and a couple of others had us holed up."

"Us?" Cummings demanded, then he saw Doll who had come through the door, and he turned accusing eyes on Rod. "Of all the chuckle-headed idiots, you take the cake with the pink icing. What'd you drag Doll into your ruckus for?"

"He didn't," Doll said quickly. "I came without invitation. He couldn't get rid of me."

"I could have, if'n it had been me," the old man snapped. "I'd have warmed up your behind and sent you packing."

Kane, his face sullen, burst out, "Devers, are you sure it was Abbot? Did you see him?"

"Hell no. But who else could it be? Larkin, maybe?"

Kane, plainly troubled by this, shook his head. "No, not Otto. It wasn't any of us." He motioned to Cummings. "Clay told us what Mrs. Nance heard Shannon say in the store." He swallowed, fighting his natural stubbornness, then he burst out, "We got no reason to like you, Devers, going over to Hermann like you done, but we didn't swallow the yarn about you rustling our calves."

"Sounds like you heard it," Rod said.

"Tell him the rest of it," Cummings said.

Kane gripped the saddle horn with a big hand. "We had a meeting a couple of nights ago. Shannon claimed you'd been slapping your brand on some of his calves and a couple of mine, but nobody believes him and he didn't show us no proof. Abbot wanted us to hit Spade, but we decided to wait till Hermann made a move."

"You're talking different than you were," Rod said.

Cummings laughed. "There's a reason for that, too."

"It's our wives," Kane said, red-faced. "Mrs. Larkin was sore because Otto wasn't with her when the baby came, and Mrs. Kane said she'd had enough of meetings and fight talk until we knew we had something to fight about."

Cummings dismounted. "I've been talking to him most of the night. I keep telling him Hermann didn't come here to grab any of the north valley range, but he's hard to convince. Hermann's sore about getting his windows shot out, so I told Sam he'd best ride to Spade and have a talk with Hermann."

"I ain't riding to Spade," Kane said. "If he wants to talk, he can come to town."

"He had a hell of a reception the day he got to town," Rod said.

"Yeah," Kane muttered. "Maybe we was wrong, listening to Abbot. If we knew for sure he was the one who was throwing lead at you all night . . ."

"You said it wasn't any of your bunch," Rod shouted. "Who the hell's left?"

Kane lowered his gaze. "If you don't know, I ain't telling you."

He was still thinking of George. It was typical of him. Once his mind was made up, nothing short of a miracle could change it. He was still afraid of Hermann. The fear had been in him too long, planted and watered by Abbot's sly words, so long that even if he and his neighbors broke with Abbot, they would still suspect Hermann of trickery.

Doll had started a fire in the stove. Now she appeared in the doorway, calling, "Get down and come in, Mr. Kane. I'll have breakfast for all of you in a few minutes."

"I'd best get back home," Kane said. "Mrs. Kane is fretting a lot these days, but thank you kindly."

"We ain't settled nothing, Sam," Cummings said. "You coming to Spade or not?"

"No," Kane said. "We'll talk to him if he comes to town, though I don't figure any good will come of talk."

He wheeled his horse and rode away. Cummings swore. "Stubborn as hell, that gent. Ain't no skin off my nose. Don't know why I'm into this." He shrugged, then grinned at Rod. "So you had quite a night."

"Quite a night," Rod agreed. "How'd you get Sam to ride over here with you?"

"We heard the shooting," Cummings said, "and I figured you were in trouble. I thought maybe we'd get the deadwood on Abbot."

"Looks like he was afraid you would."

Cummings nodded. "Never thought of him hearing us and sloping out like that. Well, I'll put my horse up. I'm about ready for that breakfast of Doll's."

Rod walked across the yard with Cummings, thinking that

Kane had come to find out who was doing the shooting, but not believing it was Abbot. He had trusted the horse trader so long that it was natural to want to trust him now, natural for him to hope that events would prove his judgment right.

"I came up here to get Abbot," Rod said as Cummings pulled gear from his mount. "I knew damned well he'd show up, but I couldn't do anything with Doll here."

"What would you have done if Doll hadn't been here?" Cummings demanded.

"I'd have gone after him before it was daylight," Rod said. "I'd have killed him. Nothing's going to be right on this range until he's dead."

Cummings gave him a studying stare. "You should have done it before. You've been too easy, Rod. You're too easy on Doll, too."

Rod said nothing to that, but he thought irritably that Cummings was the last man in the valley to advise him about a woman. When they returned to the cabin Doll had breakfast ready. After they finished eating, Rod said, "You take Doll back to Spade, Clay. She'll be safer there than in town."

"You're taking her," Clay said. "You can't stay here."

"You mean I can't leave here," Rod said. "They'll burn me out if I leave."

Cummings shook his head. "That's where you're wrong. Abbot will try something else next time. If he burns you out now, he'll throw Kane on your side."

Rod didn't believe that. But after he thought about it, he realized he couldn't let Doll and Cummings go alone, not with Doll afraid of Abbot as she was. Besides, he wanted to be with Doll when Hermann saw her again. He still did not understand why Hermann had called her Marcia and fainted unless he thought she was his daughter. He wondered if the thought had occurred to Doll.

"Is there any hurry about going back?" Doll asked. "I'm awfully tired."

"I could stand a snooze myself," Cummings said.

Doll tried to smile, weariness showing in the droop of her shoulders. "I'll lie down for an hour, Rod, but I think I ought to go to town."

"No, we'd best go to Spade," Cummings said. "Marcia will be all right, if that's what's worrying you."

Doll nodded and let it go, not feeling like arguing. Rod went outside and lay down on the shady side of the cabin. He tried to guess what Abbot's next move would be, but he fell asleep at once, and when Cummings shook him awake, he found it hard to believe he had been asleep at all.

"Time we was moving," Cummings said.

Rod sat up and rubbed his eyes. "Did Hermann come out of it after we left?"

"Yeah, he's all right, but Grace was scared to death. Hermann wouldn't talk in front of her, and I had to leave 'cause I wanted to get up here last night, so I didn't find out why he fainted when he saw Doll. But there was some reason for it. You can bet on that."

They saddled up and rode south, hitting the creek two miles above Poplar City. Because Doll was worried about her mother, Cummings left them and went into town. He caught up with them when they struck the road as it bent south around the lake.

"Your ma's all right," Cummings said.

Doll nodded, too tired to question him. Rod, glancing at the old man, sensed that something had passed between him and Marcia that he wasn't telling. Perhaps she hadn't wanted Doll to go to Spade, and Cummings had refused to send Doll back to town.

The sun was far down in the west when they reined up beside the poplars in front of the Spade ranch house. Juan Herrara came toward them, giving them his toothy grin. Rod would have helped with the horses if George had not called from the house, "Rod, Mr. Hermann wants to see you. You, too, Clay."

When they went into the house Hermann was lying on the couch, Grace seated beside him. She rose, angry eyes on Doll. She asked sharply, "Why did you bring her back, Rod?"

"I don't have to stay . . ." Doll began.

"She's welcome here," Hermann said harshly. "Go upstairs, Grace."

She hesitated, her face shrewish in the slanting sunlight coming through the open door. Suddenly she whirled and crossed the room to the stairs. She climbed them, her heels striking each step with staccato sharpness in the manner of a child giving vent to her temper.

"Do any good, Clay?" Hermann asked.

"They'll meet you in town," Cummings answered.

Hermann's eyes turned to the windows that had been shot out when Abbot and his men had made their attack. He wasn't sure of himself, Rod thought, and he still wasn't convinced that the assailants had not represented the north valley men.

"I don't know," Hermann said. "I've never been up against anything like this before. Maybe it won't do any good to talk to them." He pinned his eyes on Doll, smiling a little. "Come here."

He was sick, Rod saw, and all at once his years had caught up with him. Doll hesitated, then reluctantly moved to the couch. Reaching out, Hermann took her hand. He said softly, "Doll, I have every reason to think you are my daughter."

Doll jerked her hand back as if repelled by what he had said. She whirled and ran to Rod. He put his arms around her and shook his head at Hermann. He said, "We were damned near killed last night. Now we're tired and hungry and mighty near the end of our twine."

"Who would want to kill you?" Hermann asked.

"Abbot and Chuck England." Rod looked at George. "And Todd Shannon."

George's face was expressionless. He said, "I'll have Wang fix something for you to eat," and left the room.

Hermann moistened his colorless lips with the tip of his tongue. "Doll, I didn't know your mother was in the valley. I hurt her a long time ago. Maybe I can make it up to her now."

Doll drew away from Rod, her eyes hating Hermann. She said with biting contempt, "I'm not your daughter. Let my mother alone."

Hermann sat up, plainly shocked by the way Doll had spoken to him. "I would be the last person in the world to defend myself, but I have the right to make amends."

"How can anyone make amends for . . . for what you did?" Doll cried.

Rod put an arm around her waist. "Talk to her in the morning," he said, and led her into the dining room.

Rod went to the bunkhouse as soon as he had eaten, George promising to take Doll upstairs to a bedroom. Rod lay down on his bunk and was asleep at once. It seemed only a moment later that Cummings was shaking him awake and Rod saw that it was dawn.

"Roll out," Cummings said excitedly. "We've got more trouble than you ever dreamed about. Marcia said Abbot had an ace up his sleeve, but she didn't say what it was. Maybe she didn't know."

Rod put his feet on the floor, fully awake now. "What are you talking about?"

"Somebody blowed the sand reef last night and water's pouring through the hole like a mill race. We'll have the marginal land around the lake exposed and Kane and his neighbors will move onto it. What do you think Hermann's gonna do about that?"

Rod stared at the old man's face. "I can guess," he said. "We'll have hell to pay now."

Chapter XVIII

Rod BUCKLED his gun belt around him, put on his hat, and went outside to the horse trough. He washed his face, thinking that he should have foreseen this. Cummings was right. Kane and his neighbors would leave their places to grab the marginal land and Hermann wouldn't stand for it. Abbot wanted to promote a fight. Well, this was the one move that should turn the trick.

"You wake George?" Rod asked Cummings.

"Yeah, I woke him. He said he'd get Hermann up."

As they turned toward the house, Rod asked, "How'd you find out?"

"Something woke me. I thought I heard an explosion, so I got my horse and crossed the bridge. Hell, I was in water up to my horse's belly before I knew it."

A lamp had been lighted in the living room, and as Rod went into the house, he saw Hermann coming down the stairs, Doll and Grace behind him. When he saw Cummings, he called, "What's this all about, Clay?"

"You've got trouble," Cummings snapped. "It's up to you now."

George called from the dining room, "Wang's got breakfast ready."

Hermann tramped across the living room, the girls still behind him, Doll worried and Grace sleepy and indifferent. Hermann said over his shoulder, "George says somebody blowed a channel in the sand reef."

"That's right," Cummings said. "You'll have a few thousand acres of new land in a few hours and the little fry will move onto it as soon as they hear. That's why I said it was up to you."

Hermann sat down at the table and drank the scalding coffee the cook placed before him. He wiped a hand across his mouth. "One way to wake up is to boil your gullet." He yawned loudly. "Well, I don't see anything to get excited about. I own the lake shore, so the land's mine. Ever hear of riparian right, Clay?"

"Yeah, I've heard of it," Cummings snapped, "but legal she-nanigans ain't gonna settle this."

"I figure it will," Hermann said.

Cummings sat down across from Hermann. "I ain't got no ax to grind, but I've been willing to help out just to keep a fight from boiling up." He nodded at Rod who was already seated beside Doll. "You talk to him. I'm out of it."

"I don't have any ax to grind, either," Rod said. "I was hired to protect Hermann, but if he's bound to make a fight out of it, then I'm done, too."

Hermann reared back, scowling. "Damn it, the land's mine. There's no question about it."

George pulled a chair back and sat down beside Grace. He said, "Mr. Hermann, the question right now isn't who owns the land. In time the courts will decide that, and I'm not sure you can make your claim stick."

Angry now, Hermann said, "I know I can. As long as I own the shore line, any lake bottom that's exposed belongs to me."

Wang brought a platter of flapjacks and bacon and padded back to the kitchen for the coffee pot. George glanced at Grace who seemed to have little interest either way. He sighed. "Rod, tell Mr. Hermann what we're up against."

This was as good a time as any to have it out with George, Rod thought. He pinned his eyes on his brother. "You didn't tell me all there was to tell when you hired me."

Startled, George said, "What didn't I tell you?"

"About Todd Shannon."

Hermann looked up from his plate. "What's this?"

George stared at Rod, momentarily shaken. He said in a low tone, "Before I hired Rod, I made a deal to buy information from Shannon. I had to know what was going on in the valley and it was the only thing I could think of."

"You can't trust Shannon," Rod said bitterly. "Nobody can. He'd sell his own mother out for a dime."

"It was the best I could do," George said. "With Mr. Her-mann coming to the valley, I had to do something."

Rod let it go, deciding this was no time to push it. He turned to Hermann. "If you try to keep Kane and his bunch from mov-ing onto the marginal land, you'll have a fight whether you want it or not. Words won't convince 'em you want to be a good neighbor. Actions will."

Hermann pounded the table, his face red. "I won't give them land that belongs to me. I saw what the situation was the day we came to the valley. With that marginal land drained and planted to grass, I can double Spade's herd."

"That's right," Rod said, "but it ain't got a damned thing to do with this. You've got two choices. You can tell these men they're welcome to settle on land that you don't need. If you do, you'll make friends and you'll cut the ground out from under Abbot. If you don't, you'd best call your boys in off the range, give 'em guns, and tell 'em to shoot every man who crosses your north line."

Silence then while everybody but Hermann ate, their eyes on their plates. Hermann looked around the table, his face more purple than red, then slowly the color drained out of it. He breathed, "Grace, what do you think?"

She looked up. "You don't need the land."

"You're sore about getting your windows shot out the other night," Rod said, "and that's exactly why Abbot done it. I've heard a lot of hogwash since you came here about your principle of avoiding trouble even if it cost you money. That's all it was, I reckon. Just hogwash."

"Let them have it, Mr. Hermann," George said. "Abbot was counting on you claiming the land, or he wouldn't have blown a channel in the reef."

"You can bet your bottom dollar they know about it." Cummings said. "Chances are they're on their way to town now."

Hermann shook his head as he reached for the flapjacks. He ate, the silence tight and oppressive. He knew, Rod told himself, that everyone here at the table was against him, even Grace, but he was a stubborn man.

Rod glanced at Doll who reached under the table and took his hand, giving him a small smile. He winked at her covertly, thinking that he must have appeared to her and Marcia as stubborn and bullheaded as Karl Hermann was appearing to him now. He turned his head quickly, realizing that Grace was watching him, plainly amused.

George broke the silence with, "Mr. Hermann, you have only one choice to make. I know what it is to be a poor man and want to get ahead. Rod knows it better than I do because he had the guts to make his own way. I wish I had."

Hermann was hit hard by that. He said, "George, you've got everything."

"Not quite," George said harshly. "If you're so damned greedy you're going to hold this marginal land you don't need, you'd better start looking for a new superintendent."

Surprised, Rod stared at George, sensing a tough, unbending

quality in his brother he had not realized was there. Grace was as surprised as Rod. Impulsively she bent toward George and ran her arm through his. She said, "I'm proud of you, honey."

"I'll give you a job on the Rocking R," Rod said.

George gave him a tight grin. "I'll remember that."

Cummings rose and kicked back his chair. "I'm going home. Go ahead and have your fight. I sure wasted my time and a night's sleep when I went to see Sam Kane."

Rod got up. "We might as well ride back to town, Doll."

Doll had not said anything through the meal. Now she rose and stood beside Rod, accusing eyes on Hermann. She said, "Men like Sam Kane may be mistaken, but they don't deserve to die because of their mistakes. Remember that when you order their deaths."

Hermann was looking at her, hands clutching the table so tightly that his knuckles were white. He whispered, "You, too." Then he rose, hands still on the table. In two sentences Doll accomplished what the rest of them had failed to do with all their talking. "I won't order anyone's death, Doll. The land isn't worth it."

"Then we'd better start for town," Rod said. "You've been wanting to talk to the little fellows. If I'm guessing right, you'll get your chance today."

"Harness my team, George," Hermann said. "I'll take the buggy."

Rod left the dining room with Doll. She said, "I want to go upstairs a minute. I'll be right down."

"I'll saddle up," Rod said, and started to follow George and Cummings out of the house.

"Rod."

He turned. Grace stood in the doorway of the dining room, giving him a faint smile, her hands knotted at her sides. He said, "Well?"

"It's funny, Rod," she said in a low voice. "Funny how things work one way when you try so hard to make them work the opposite. You're going to marry Doll, aren't you?"

He nodded. "If she'll take me."

"She'll take you," Grace said. "All you have to do is to look at her and see that she loves you. Well, you're two of a kind. Nesters."

"I guess we are," he said, sensing the bitterness that was in her.

"I'm going to marry George," Grace told him. "I guess we're two of a kind, too."

"He's a good man," Rod said. "I didn't know how good a man until this morning."

He left the house then, not looking back. Later when he rode north with Doll beside him, Hermann following in his buggy and George on a horse, he wondered if Grace would stay here at Spade. Probably not, he thought. She'd take George to San Francisco with her. In time he would stand where Karl Hermann stood now, and maybe that was what he wanted, but at least he would be his own man. This morning he had stood against Hermann, probably for the first time since he had gone to work for him. It would not be the last time.

They put their horses through the swift water that was boiling through the break in the sand reef, and went on, following the road around the north shore of the lake. Rod thought he knew what had happened. Abbot had sent a man, probably England, to blow the channel through the reef and at the same time had sent Shannon to tell Sam Kane the water had broken through.

Kane would get his neighbors together and they'd head south to claim the marginal land. Abbot could count on that with the same certainty he could be sure that spring would follow winter. Kane and the rest would be armed and on the prod. But Abbot was making one mistake. He hadn't considered the possibility that Hermann would not resist.

The danger lay in the fact that Kane and his neighbors would expect to fight. Trouble might start before Hermann had a chance to open his mouth. But maybe not if Kane was the leader. His wife had cooled him down. She was probably the only person who could have.

Rod wished that Doll wasn't with them. He glanced at her, wondering if he could get her to go back to Spade, or at least leave the road so she wouldn't be with them if they met the north valley men. No use to ask her, he decided. She'd say what she had at the cabin, that a woman should face danger with the man she loved.

They were within a mile of town when Doll said, "They're coming."

Rod nodded, saying nothing. He had seen them before she had, a dozen or more riders coming fast. At this distance Rod could not tell whether Abbot was with them or not. Abbot's natural tendency was to slide out of the way before trouble started, so it seemed a good guess he wouldn't be along. But this might be different. He was playing his high ace.

Rod hipped around in the saddle to look at Hermann. He said, "I'll start the talking," and Hermann nodded agreement. He turned back, lifting his gun from his holster and dropping it. The incoming riders were close enough now for him to recognize them. Abbot wasn't with them. Neither was England or Shannon.

Rod's first feeling was one of relief. It changed at once to concern as he reined up and motioned for the others to stop. Now he could see Kane's face, as hard as chiseled stone. The old familiar stubbornness was in him.

All of them were armed just as they had been the day the Hermanns had come to the valley, but there was a difference, intangible but very real. They were going through regardless. The possibility they could get what they wanted without fighting had not occurred to them.

"Start riding," Rod told Doll. "Go on to town."

But she shook her head at him, refusing to move, and then it was too late. Kane stopped, holding up his hand as a signal to the others, and his great, overbearing voice rolled out of him, "Get out of the way, Hermann. No damned millionaire is keeping us off land that don't belong to him." He lifted his rifle to cover Hermann. "We'll blast our way through if we have to, and that's a promise."

Chapter XIX

THERE MUST be an end to waiting, Marcia thought dully as Clay Cummings left the hotel after telling her about Rod and Doll holding Rod's cabin against Abbot and his men. She had begged Cummings to send Doll to town and he had refused.

"Come to Spade if you want her," Cummings had said.

But she couldn't do that and she was sure Cummings knew it. She wanted to scream at him that he was butting into something that was none of his business, but she didn't. Clay had picked his side. He had nothing to gain, but he had taken chips in the game because he liked Karl Hermann and he thoroughly disliked Jason Abbot. He liked Rod, too. And Doll. Maybe he knew what he was doing.

Of all the men in the country, Cummings was the only one who stood outside the tangle of trouble. For that reason she trusted him. He had taken some risk when he had ridden into town to let her know that Doll and Rod were safe. Abbot, desperate now, might kill him if they met. Cummings had never let anyone doubt where he stood.

But if Abbot was in town, he stayed off the street. Marcia watched Cummings mount and ride south, intuitively knowing that from now on nothing would be the same again. Abbot had forced the issue last night. Rod would kill him the next time they met. Abbot must know that. But what would he do?

Marcia went back along the hall to her bedroom, leaving Ada to take care of the kitchen and dining room and to look into the lobby occasionally. She knew Ada resented it, but right now she didn't care. Ada might grumble, but she wouldn't quit.

It wasn't until Marcia was in her bedroom that she realized she was sick. She was terribly hot, then she was chilled. But nothing was wrong with her, she told herself as she lay down. She'd be all right if Doll were here.

Marcia realized she was being selfish. She wanted Doll with her. Then, slowly, her mind brought all of this into focus and she realized Doll was safer on Spade than she would be in town. Abbot couldn't touch her as long as she was there, but she would be in danger if she were in town, for he was the kind who would destroy something he could not have for himself.

Of all the crazy twists his mind had taken, wanting Doll was the craziest and the worst. Queer, she thought, that she hadn't sensed it a long time ago. It explained some things she had not understood, particularly his unreasonable hatred for Rod. Abbot would hate anything and anybody who stood between him and Doll, and that included her as well as Rod.

Marcia had lived in a hell of regret for days. Now there was just a dull emptiness in her. It was stupid to go on blaming herself. What was past was past and only the future could be shaped. But she had no future, not after what she had done in bringing this trouble to the valley.

When it was over, she would try to put the broken pieces together, but she would fail. Doll would never feel quite the same toward her again. If any good had come out of these last hectic hours, it was that Doll and Rod had found each other again. At least she hoped they had, yet the thought brought its pain, too.

All this time she had wanted Doll and Rod to leave the country, to get married. She had wanted Rod to be responsible for Doll's safety. Now she realized she hadn't thought it through. Her life had been focused on Doll so much that without her, there was nothing left. She couldn't share Doll with anyone, not even Rod.

She put a hand to her throbbing head, knowing she wasn't thinking clearly. You can't want two contrary things at the same time, and that was what she had been wanting. Then she told herself Doll would never be happy without Rod.

She sat up, realizing it was dark. She had been thinking crazy, morbid thoughts, and back of them was Karl Hermann. She found it hard to believe it had happened so long ago. She had loved Hermann; she had been young and full of dreams, and he had destroyed them.

He was the first man she had ever known. Nothing had been right after that; no man had ever satisfied her. She was probably like all women. No, that was wrong. Doll was different. She would make something out of her life, find some meaning that had always eluded Marcia.

The thought steadied her. She lighted a lamp and went into her parlor. When she glanced at the clock she was surprised at the hour. It was after midnight. Perhaps she had slept part of that time, although she didn't remember sleeping.

She found paper and pen and ink, and pulled a chair up to her table. The pillow case she had been working on so long was in front of her. She pushed it aside impatiently, wondering why she hadn't thrown it away weeks ago.

Again time slipped by while she stared at the paper. She wanted to write something to Doll. It would be better for everyone if she left the valley. Rod would look after Doll. But he might be killed. No, she had to stay until this was settled.

She thought of Hermann in a detached way that surprised her. She had wondered for years what her feeling would be if she saw him again. She had seen him the day he had come to the valley and she had wondered why she had ever loved him.

He wasn't worth loving. Or hating. A pudgy, middle-aged man, sort of tired-looking. If she had seen him months ago, this wouldn't have happened. All these years she had been driven by a bitter hatred that had been fed by a girl's destroyed dreams. It must not happen to Doll.

She began to write in a shaky hand she could not seem to control. "Doll, listen to your heart." She stopped, unable to think of anything else, her mind turning back to her past and the mistakes she'd made.

She had met men she could have loved if she had let herself. Oh, it wouldn't have been the best kind of life. She would probably have lived the way Mrs. Larkin was living, but Mrs. Larkin seemed happy. Apparently poverty and annual child-bearing were what she expected.

Marcia folded the paper and put it into the pocket of her dress. She'd finish it later. Or throw it away. She'd probably see Doll in the morning anyhow. Then a restlessness possessed her and she rose and blew out the lamp.

She walked down the dark hall to the lobby, lighted by the bracket lamp above the desk. She went on out into the street, totally dark except for the pale light from the lobby window behind her. The town was asleep and silent, the false fronts an uneven line against the sky.

More waiting. And for what? She didn't know, but she wasn't sick now. Just tense with the waiting. For tomorrow. Or the next tomorrow when trouble would come and guns would sound and men would die. She might die, too, but the thought did not bother her. There was peace in death, and she had not known peace for a long time.

She had always shown the world a composed face; she had forced herself to be practical, and she had made her way. She had survived and she had raised Doll. The thought gave her comfort.

She took the bracket lamp down from the wall and went into the dining room. Ada had left it clean and neat as she always did, but Marcia was surprised when she went into the kitchen. Dirty dishes covered the table and back of the range. Ada had given up and gone to bed.

Marcia built a fire and heated water. It was dawn when the kitchen was cleaned up. She thought she was hungry, but when she made coffee and fried bacon and eggs, she found it hard to eat. She drank two cups of coffee, carried the lamp into her bedroom and lay down.

She didn't think she would sleep, but she did, and it was well into the morning when the door squealed as it was shoved open. She sat up, blinking. Abbot stood there, tall and immaculate and smiling with cool, malicious confidence.

"Sleeping with your clothes on," he said disapprovingly. "What happened?"

She rose and blew out the lamp that had been burning all this time. She said, "Never come into my bedroom again. Do you understand that?"

"You're independent as hell," he said harshly. "It won't do. Where would you be if I took this hotel away from you?"

She said, "Come with me," and brushing past him, crossed the hall into the parlor. The waiting would soon be over, for now there was no doubt in her mind about what she must do.

Abbot followed her. He said, "You've got a way out, you know."

She moved to the table and turned to face him, knowing he meant Doll. "I don't owe you anything, Jason. If you try to take the hotel, I'll go to court and tell how I've repaid you."

Shocked, he said, "You've always had some pride. About us."

"Not any more. All I have is shame."

"Then you'd best think about Doll," he said roughly.

She stood within a foot of the drawer that held her gun, but there was no hurry. She wondered how he could be so confident with Rod alive. She said, "Rod will kill you."

He grinned at her, his confidence unshaken. "I'm not worried. Last night we blew the reef out and it won't be long until a lot of the lake bottom will be exposed. Todd Shannon let Kane know. They'll move onto it, Kane and Larkin and all of them, and you know what Hermann will do. Nothing can stop a fight now, and this time Hermann and Devers will be killed."

For a moment she stared at him, understanding now why he was so sure of himself. It was inconceivable that Hermann would give the land up. That was the only chance there was of avoiding the fight Abbot had worked so hard to provoke.

She had planned to kill him, but if he had not told her this, she might have failed to find the courage it took. She had it now. She would stop the trouble, if killing Abbot would stop it.

She whirled to the table and yanked the drawer open; she turned to face him, the gun in her hand, and then in a rush of panic she knew she was too late. He must have expected this, for he had drawn his gun.

She felt the numbing impact of the bullet and she went down, the sound of the shot hammering against her ears, terribly loud here in the confines of the room. She lay there, her eyes closed, a great weight upon her chest so that it was hard to breathe.

She was dying and she didn't really care. No more waiting or worry or nagging sense of guilt. She must have known all the time that it would be her last morning, or she wouldn't have started to write the note to Doll. But she hadn't finished it. She wished she could see Doll before she went.

Chapter XX

Sam Kane could not have said anything that was more completely wrong than to order Karl Hermann to get out of his way. They were on Spade grass, well past the sign that Clay Cummings had put up years ago, so it was Kane and the little ranchers who were trespassing. And then to have a rifle pointed at him was too much.

Rod was to do the talking, but Hermann forgot that. He reared back, the rage that had been smoldering in him since the night the windows of Spade's ranch house had been shot out now bursting into flames. He bellowed, "What right have you got on this grass? You saw the sign. Get to hell off Spade range."

Rod swung his horse directly between Kane and Hermann. He said to Hermann, "Are you gonna let me do the talking or not?"

"What good is talking?" Kane shouted. "I told . . ."

"Sam," Rod broke in, "talking is real good right now if your life is any good. You pull the trigger of that Winchester and you're a dead man. Before your neighbors could cut me down, I'd drill Larkin through the brisket. I ain't bragging. I know what I can do."

His words sobered them. Even Kane, stubborn and belligerent, blinked his eyes, the barrel of his rifle sloping downward. Hermann laughed shortly. He said, "That's better, friend. I came to this valley without any thought of stealing grass that wasn't mine, but it seems like you boys have tried me and convicted me before I had a chance to talk to you."

"He wanted to talk the day he got here," Rod said. "Remember that, Sam?"

"And then some of you ride in after dark and shoot the windows out of my house," Hermann said ominously. "That's a hell . . ."

"We didn't do no such thing," Larkin broke in. "The truth is Abbot wanted us to get together and wipe you out while your hands were gone from the home ranch, but we wouldn't do it."

137

Rod, glancing at Hermann, saw that doubt was in his mind, for Larkin's denial substantiated what Rod had told him at the time. If he believed these men were innocent of that raid, he would feel better about giving them the marginal land.

"If it wasn't any of you boys," Rod said, "it must have been Abbot, England, and Shannon. There were three of them."

"Reckon it was," Kane muttered. "All we know is it wasn't us."

"Now if you've got down off your high horse, Sam," Rod said, "maybe we can talk a little sense. You heard about the sand reef going out?"

"You know damned well we did," Kane shouted, suddenly angry again. "What do you think we're here for?"

"I figured that's why you were here, all right," Rod said, "but what you didn't know was that Abbot blew a channel in the reef and sent somebody to tell you the water had broken through. He figured you'd come helling down here just like you're doing and we'd have a fight, which is what he's been trying to work from the start."

"Got any proof?" Kane snapped.

"Good enough for me. Who told you, Shannon?"

Kane nodded. "Yeah, it was Shannon. Got to my place about midnight. Said if we wanted that marginal land, we'd better get on it."

"The water broke through after that," Rod said. "Not long before dawn. Cummings heard an explosion. You can believe that or not, Sam, but there's one thing that will prove what I'm saying even to a bullhead like you. Leastwise it'll prove you've got no cause to get on the prod. Hermann here ain't figuring on stopping you from taking the marginal land if you want it."

Kane's mouth fell open, eyes instinctively turning to Hermann. This was the last thing he expected to hear. It was the same with Larkin and the others.

Hermann nodded reluctantly. "By riparian right, the exposed lake bottom is mine, but it isn't worth fighting for. Spade has all the grass it needs. If you want the lake bottom, take it. I'm going back to San Francisco in a few days, but I'm leaving orders with George Devers to give you any help you need."

"I suggest you go back to Spade with Mr. Hermann," George said, "and draw up an agreement to that effect."

Kane licked his lips, gaze turning to Larkin. All of them looked ashamed, like kids who had been trying to do something on the sly that was forbidden, only to find out there was nothing to keep them from doing it in the open.

"I'll be damned," Kane said. "Maybe we had you pegged wrong, Mr. Hermann."

"Now maybe you did," Hermann said, good humor flowing back into him.

He looked at Doll, seeking her approval, and when she smiled at him, he smiled back, and Rod, watching, sensed that he had made this concession for her, still believing she was his daughter. Then Rod was aware that Larkin had ridden forward, bringing his horse in alongside Rod's.

"There's some kind of trouble in town," Larkin said in a low voice. "We heard a shot in the hotel. I wanted to look into it, but Sam, he said we didn't have time. Wasn't any of our business, anyhow, so we came on."

A shot! Marcia was in the hotel. Abbot would be in town, waiting for news of the fight that he would be sure had developed before now. Rod took a long, ragged breath, staring at Larkin's thin, worried face. Marcia had created a monster who had destroyed her, or she had destroyed him, believing it was the only way to prevent the trouble that she had started.

"You go on to Spade," Rod said. "I'll look into it."

He cracked steel to his sorrel, not looking at Doll, and not wanting her to go with him, but afraid to try to make her stay. He heard Doll call to him, but he didn't stop. He rode past Kane and through the line of ranchers, glimpsing their startled, questioning faces.

He kept his horse in a run all the way to town. Before he reached it, he thought of a dozen things that might have happened, all of them bad. Rod pulled up in front of the hotel and stepped down, leaving the reins dangling. He heard a horse, and looking back, saw Doll coming, slashing her horse with her quirt at every jump.

No one was on the street, no horses racked at the hitch poles. Rod ran into the lobby, his gun in his hand. The room was empty. He looked into the dining room. It was empty. By the time he reached the door that opened from the lobby into the hall, he saw Ada Larkin running toward him.

"Where's Marcia?" Rod demanded, dropping his gun into holster.

Ada didn't say anything until she reached him. She was scared and trembling, and it took a moment for her to say, "In her room. Abbot shot her. I can't find the doctor."

"Doll's coming. Keep her out here for a minute," and Rod ran on down the hall to Marcia's bedroom.

She lay on her bed, face turned toward the door, and he

knew at once she recognized him. He took off his hat and walked slowly to the bed. She reached out for his hand and gripped it.

"I'm so glad you came, Rod," Marcia whispered. "I've been praying that you would. And Doll."

"She's coming," Rod said, and sat down on the edge of the bed.

Marcia didn't have long. Blood made a dark stain on her dress below her left shoulder. She squeezed his hand, peering at him as if she found it hard to see him even at this short distance. She whispered, "Can you hear me, Rod?"

"I'm right here, Marcia," he said gently.

"I'm not leaving Doll anything but a bad name. She loves you. Promise me you'll take care of her."

For a moment he was too choked up to say anything. He had always liked Marcia, and even now, knowing what she had done, he still liked her. But she was dying and there was nothing he could do.

She squeezed his hand again. "I brought all this trouble on you, Rod. Can you forgive me?"

"Of course," he said. "I'll take care of Doll. I promise."

Her hand dropped away from his. "I tried to kill Abbot. That's why he shot me. I made him what he was, Rod. God forgive me, but I didn't know I'd bring so much misery to so many people by trying to get even with Hermann."

She smiled a little, and she seemed contented as if the pain had gone and she was at peace. He asked, "Marcia, is Doll Hermann's daughter?"

"No. After Hermann left me I married a man named Ted Nance. He died a few months later and I've had to fight for a living since then." Her eyes closed. "Rod, be good to Doll."

He rose and left the room. Doll was in the hall talking to Ada in a low tone. Ada had her arms around her and she was crying. Rod said, "Come in, Doll," and walking past the two girls, went down the hall and across the lobby and into the street.

For a moment he stood in front of the hotel, the morning sun sharp and bright on the white dust. If anyone was to blame, he thought, it was Karl Hermann who wanted at this late hour to make amends. Rod was glad Doll was not his daughter. He probably would never see Hermann again. He hoped he wouldn't. If he did, he would say and probably do something he would be sorry for later. No good could be done that way; the past was written in the book and there was no changing it. All he could do now was to get Jason Abbot.

He looked at the Palace, wondering if the man was there. He was sure Abbot would not leave town until he heard about the fight. There was only one thing to do, hunt him down and kill him as he would a mad dog. He wished he had killed him that night at the Rocking R.

Rod went into the saloon. He asked the barkeep, "Have you seen Abbot?"

The barman looked at his hard, set face and shook his head. "Not today."

"If you're hiding him," Rod said, "I'll be back."

"I wouldn't hide the ornery son," the barkeep said. "He's not here, I tell you."

Rod left the saloon. Abbot was probably in his office. He wouldn't fight if he could help it. Shannon and England would be around somewhere. England was the one to worry about. They might have set up a trap as they had done the day the Hermanns had come to the valley, but Rod didn't think there had been time.

He started toward Abbot's office, his gun in his hand, knowing this wasn't the smart thing to do because he was in the open. But he had no patience, no caution. Nothing was important except getting Abbot.

He watched the street windows in the little office building, but there was no movement behind the glass. He slammed the door open and went in fast. No one was here, then he heard someone going out through the back.

Rod lunged across the office to the door that led to the back room. He turned the knob and pushed; the door opened a few inches and stopped. He put his weight against it and shoved, and the door gave enough to let him through. Abbot had moved a heavy bureau against it, but he must have been alone and he hadn't had time to jam the bureau solidly against the door.

Rod ran across the room and on through the back door. He glimpsed Abbot running down the alley and threw a shot at him and missed, then the man was out of sight. Rod raced after him, not sure where Abbot had gone.

Dust that his flying feet had kicked up still hung in the air. A drug store. A vacant building. The dry goods store. A lumber yard was next. That was it, Rod thought. He was like a rat desperately trying to reach his hole. He'd find a dozen places to hide here.

A high, board fence surrounded the lumber yard. The alley gate, wide enough for a wagon to enter, was open. Again caution should have stopped Rod, but it didn't, and his recklessness very nearly cost him his life. The instant he appeared a gun roared, the bullet knocking splinters from the heavy post that anchored the gate.

Rod dived behind a pile of lumber and lay belly flat. That had been close, too close. He started crawling to the end of the pile. He couldn't stay here. If he did, Abbot would get out through the street gate and leave town. He had played his ace when he had blown the reef, but he must have realized by this time that his ace wasn't the high card, or Rod wouldn't be in town.

Rod eased around the end of the lumber pile. No one was in sight. Old Barney Fitts who ran the yard had probably left, or he might be holed up in his office. Like many others in the valley, he was in debt to Abbot, so he'd stay out of the fight, at least until he heard that Abbot had murdered Marcia.

Rod thought about that. Every man's hand except Shannon's and England's would be turned against Abbot when the story of Marcia's killing got out. He was smart enough to know that. Still, he was a schemer, and he might think he could scheme his way out of murder, once that Rod was dead. If he thought that, he'd work at this until Rod was killed, or he was.

An empty wagon was in one corner of the yard. Except for that and the small frame building that was Old Barney's office, there was nothing inside the fence except the piles of lumber. Rod swore, not knowing what to do. Abbot could be hiding behind any one of them. Rod had no way of knowing which one it was, or whether Abbot had maneuvered into a position where he could see between the boards. If he had, he'd cut loose the minute Rod showed himself.

Unexpectedly Abbot called, "Devers."

Rod didn't answer for a moment. He squatted at the corner of the lumber pile, trying to decide which pile Abbot was behind. All he could be sure of was that the man was on the far side of the yard near the street fence.

"You're a goner, Abbot," Rod called. "If I don't get you, someone else will. You'll hang for Marcia's murder."

"I didn't kill her if she's dead," Abbot flung back. "This is between you and me. You're supposed to be a gunslinger. Come and get me."

A pile of two-by-twelves lay twenty feet from Rod. He lunged toward it and dropped flat just as Abbot cut loose with two shots that missed. He shouted, "Come on, Devers. Try it again. I'll get you next time."

He probably would, Rod thought, if he could shoot that straight. He hadn't bobbed into view, so he must have lifted the ends of the boards and forced a wedge between them so he could see through the pile. There was still forty or fifty feet between him and Abbot, too far to run.

"Say your prayers, Devers," Abbot yelled. "You've got a minute to live. Maybe less. If you're coming after me, you'd better start."

Rod picked up a short end of a two-by-twelve that had been sawed from a longer piece and tossed it over the pile in front of him. Abbot laughed. "What good did that do? Come on, Devers. England's going to plug you."

Instinctively Rod glanced at the alley gate. No one was in sight. Abbot was probably trying to scare him into showing himself. He picked up another piece of wood, and reaching around the corner, started to lift the ends of two planks, intending to slip the chunk below them, but the instant his hand appeared, Abbot threw a shot that knocked splinters from the end of a board. He jerked his hand back. That was close, too.

Rod ejected the empty shell from his gun and thumbed a new load into the cylinder. Abbot taunted, "Ten seconds now, Devers. I guess you're not hell on big wheels like they say."

Rod glanced at the alley gate again. Still no one was in sight. He wished now he hadn't left the first pile of lumber. If he'd stayed there, he could have, with a little luck, reached the gate and circled the yard to the street side. Too late to think of that now. He was stuck right here.

A gun sounded from somewhere down the street. Another gun roared from the roof of the dry goods store that was next to the lumber yard, the bullet slapping into the dirt a foot from Rod's head.

He turned and looked up. England was rolling down the roof, clawing frantically at the shingles, but there was nothing to hold to. Rod shot twice, hitting him both times, and England came on off the roof, striking the ground like a sack of wheat. He didn't move.

Abbot would be momentarily diverted. Rod dived toward another pile of lumber that brought him at least twenty feet closer to where Abbot was hiding. He reached it and dropped flat just as the gun in the street opened up again.

"They've got us hipped," Todd Shannon yelled.

Rod came up to his hands and knees in time to see Shannon lurch through the street gate and fall forward. Rod didn't know who was out there, but he was opening this thing up, whoever it was. Shannon fell on his face and scrambled toward Abbot. Rod made a split second decision. An experienced gun fighter wouldn't be diverted a second time, but Abbot probably would be.

Rod jumped up and raced toward the street fence, his eyes on the pile where Abbot was hiding. Shannon yelled a warning, but not until Rod, moving at right angles to the pile of lumber, had gone far enough to see Abbot.

The man had been on his knees facing the gate, expecting someone to follow Shannon. He came around in a sort of awkward flop that took a precious second; he tilted his gun and fired, but he was scared and desperate, and the slug missed by inches. Rod shot him twice in the chest, the impact of the bullets knocking him over on his back.

Shannon yelled, "Don't shoot." He was still on his stomach, his face lifted to stare at Rod with abject fear. "I'm out of it. I didn't hurt you, Devers. I never fired a shot."

Rod moved toward him, keeping him covered, and looked down at Abbot. The man was dead. Rod suddenly felt all gone inside, now that this was finished, and for some reason he didn't hate Jason Abbot as he had. Vicious, but cheap and cowardly, too, a man who had tried to use others to do what he had lacked courage to do.

Rod looked at Shannon. "Get up."

Slowly Shannon pulled himself to his feet. Sweat ran down his face and his lips fluttered like the wings of a small, brown butterfly. He tried to say something, but his lips refused to form the words. One hand was pressed to his side where he had been shot.

"You busted my fence, didn't you, and mudded up my spring," Rod said. "You sold information to my brother, working both sides. You ain't worth a bullet."

Shannon nodded, then shook his head. "I done what Abbot told me to," he whispered. "I didn't hurt nobody."

"Get out of the valley," Rod said. "Take your family. If you don't go to work for 'em and support 'em, I'll hunt you up and blow your teeth through your head."

He turned and ran, lurching from one side to the other, wanting only to get away. It was then that Rod saw George, standing in the street gate, a gun in his hand. He asked, "All over?"

"All over," Rod said. "So it was you that got England."

George holstered his gun. "I came into town when I heard what fetched you in. I stopped at the hotel and found out about Doll's mother, then I heard the shooting, and when I started down the street, I saw England crawling up that roof, so I let him have it."

"You got him just when he was throwing down on me," Rod said. "Hell, I never thought of looking up there. He'd have got me sure if you hadn't plugged him. They must have rigged it as soon as I rode into town."

George gave him a tight grin. "Well, I'm glad I got here when I did. Shannon started running down the street when I let go at England, so I threw a shot at him. Just nicked him, looks like."

Rod held out his hand. "George, I've been wrong, but it'll be different now."

George gripped his hand and then turned away. "Yes, it'll be different," he said in a strained voice. "I'll be in San Francisco because Grace won't stay here, but you'll have the best life, Rod. If I can ever help you . . ."

"I'll remember that," Rod said.

They walked down the street together. George said, "I've been in love with Grace as long as I've known her. I couldn't help it, Rod. Can't now. Maybe it'll work out. I aim to do my part."

Rod waited until George mounted, then he said, "Tell Hermann Doll isn't his daughter. Marcia was married to a man named Ted Nance. She told me."

"I'll tell Mr. Hermann," George said, and rode away.

Rod turned into the hotel, thinking that George would call his father-in-law Mr. Hermann as long as he lived. Grace wasn't worthy of George, Rod thought, but if she was the one he wanted, it was his business. Some women did that to some men. Rod knew how it was. There would never be anyone else for him but Doll.

The door to Marcia's bedroom was closed. Doll was in the parlor standing by the window. Hearing Rod, she whirled, and when she saw who it was, she ran to him and put her arms around him, crying out, "Are you all right, Rod, are you?"

"I'm all right," he said, and held her hard against him.

"I heard the shooting." She stood with her face pressed against his shirt. "I knew I ought to go out to help you, but I couldn't, not this time."

"It was man business," he said softly.

She drew back, looking up at him. "I guess that's something I've got to learn." She held a piece of paper out to him. "Ma gave me this before she died. She couldn't talk much. I guess she wanted to write more, but that's all she got down. Maybe nothing else is important."

He looked at the words written in a shaky hand. "Doll, listen to your heart."

He nodded. "That's what's important if your heart tells you what I hope it does. I love you, Doll. I couldn't say it then, but that night in the cabin when you said a woman should face danger with the man she loves . . ." He swallowed. "Well, I guess I saw things a little straighter after that. Maybe I was wrong about putting off our marriage."

"It doesn't make any difference now, Rod," she said in a low voice. "It was just that I was so afraid of Abbot, and afraid that if I lost you, I'd have to live the way Ma did."

He put his arms around her and brought her to him again, and she began to cry. She would feel better for it, he thought. He had come a long way since Hermann's bank had taken over his father's ranch, a very long way, but he had come alone. That was the big difference. He wouldn't be alone now.

John S. Daniels was the byline adopted by Western author Wayne D. Overholser in 1952 when he began writing a most memorable and outstanding series of Western novels for J.B. Lippincott and Company, *Gunflame*, the first of these novels, was an instant success with readers and proved the first in a group of remarkable titles under this name including *The Nester* (1953), *The Land Grabbers* (1953), *The Man From Yesterday* (1957), and *Smoke of the Gun* (1958). Overholser was born in Pomeroy, Washington, and attended the University of Montana, University of Oregon, and the University of Southern California before becoming a public school teacher and principal in various Oregon communities. He began writing for Western pulp magazines in 1936 and published his first Western novel in 1948, *Buckaroo's Code*, still considered one of his best. The overriding theme in Overholser's Western fiction, including the titles published under John S. Daniels byline, is often a character's personal odyssey to find a better life and to come to terms with himself. The John S. Daniels novels tend also to amplify by this means what it was that made the American Western frontier so unique a time and place in human history. A member of both the Oregon Historical Society and the Colorado Historical Society, many of Overholser's books are set in one or another of these states. He made extensive research trips in Colorado, Montana, and Wyoming, often accompanied by his son Stephen, visiting libraries and historical sites, accumulating voluminous notes on material found in old newspapers and unpublished journals. Overholser achieves verisimilitude not by writing about "big" events in Western history, but rather by a consistently accurate evocation of the land and its people. The people, their interactions, and the land they inhabit, are the centerpieces of Overholser's fiction, and the sources of its enduring appeal.